NO LONGER PROPERTY OF
ANYTHINK LIBRARIES/
RANGEVIEW LIBRARY DISTRICT

D1442855

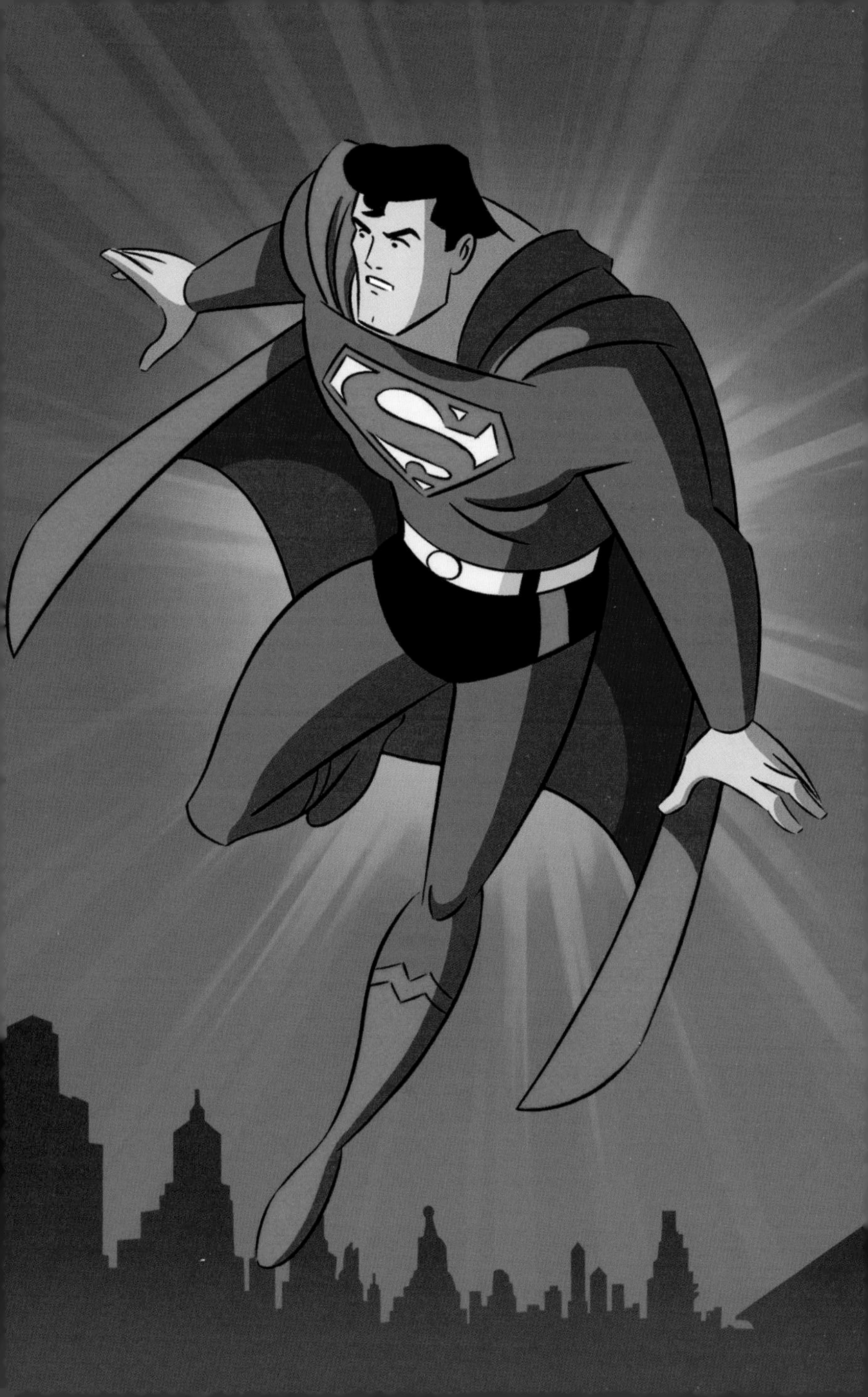

THE FUN DOESN'T STOP HERE!

DISCOVER MORE AT...
www.CAPSTONEKIDS.com

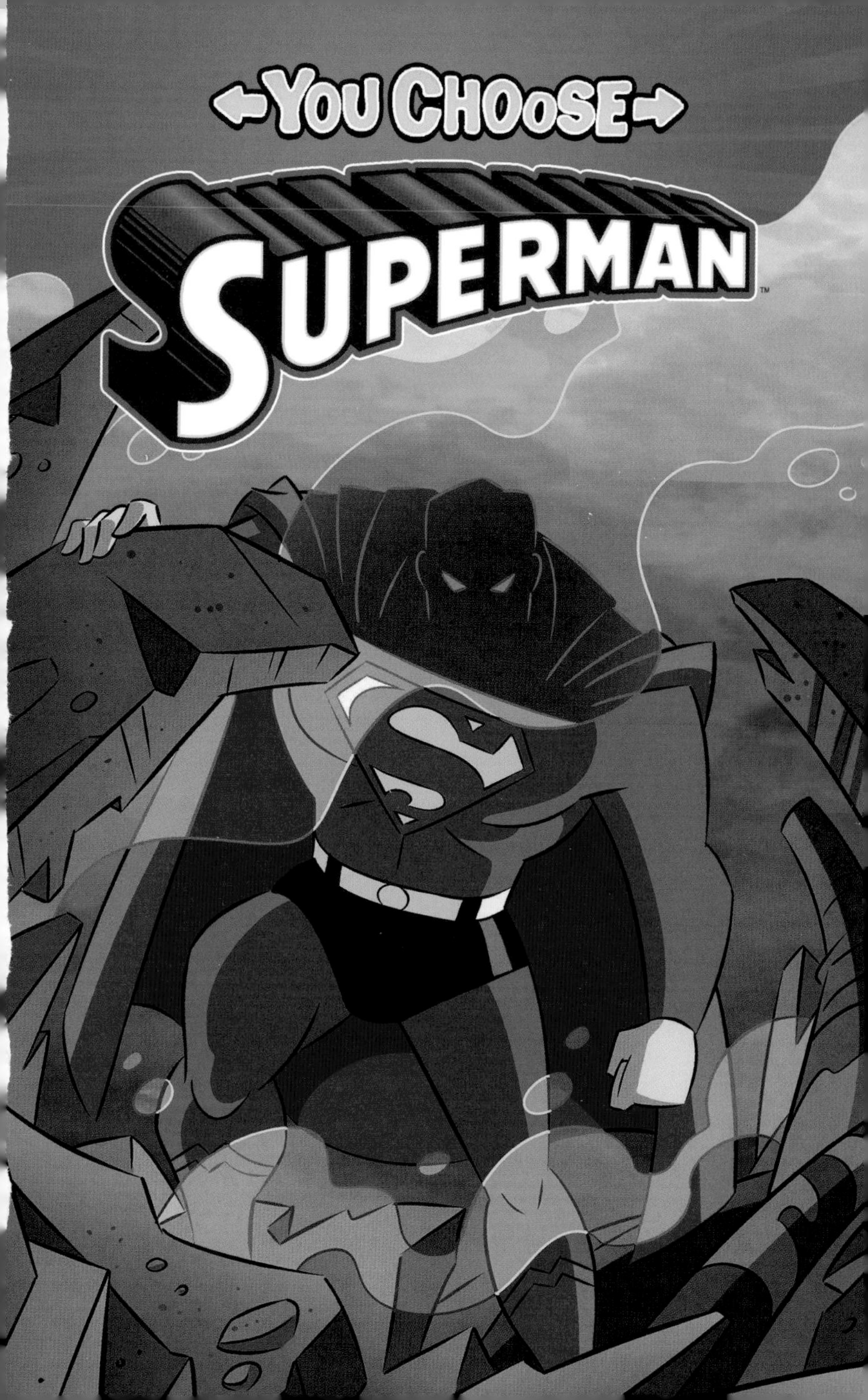
YOU CHOOSE
SUPERMAN™

You Choose Stories: Superman
is published by Stone Arch Books,
A Capstone Imprint
1710 Roe Crest Drive
North Mankato, Minnesota 56003
www.mycapstone.com

Copyright © 2018 DC Comics.
SUPERMAN and all related characters and elements are © &
™ DC Comics. WB SHIELD: ™ & © Warner Bros. Entertainment
Inc. (s18)

STAR39715

All rights reserved. No part of this publication may be
reproduced in whole or in part, or stored in a retrieval
system, or transmitted in any form or by any means,
electronic, mechanical, photocopying, recording, or
otherwise, without written permission of the publisher.

Cataloging-in-Publication Data is available
on the Library of Congress website.
ISBN: 978-1-4965-5826-8 (library binding)
ISBN: 978-1-4965-5831-2 (paperback)
ISBN: 978-1-4965-5837-4 (eBook)

Summary: When a new hero is introduced to Metropolis, he
is revealed to be one of Superman's deadliest enemies . . .
Metallo! But when he breaks free of Lex Luthor's control, he
goes on the attack. It's up to the Man of Steel to overpower
the dangerous cyborg criminal. Only you can help Superman
put a stop to the metallic menace threatening Metropolis.

Printed in the United States of America.
010830S18

METALLO ATTACKS!

Superman created by
Jerry Siegel and Joe Shuster
by special arrangement with the Jerry Siegel Family

written by
Michael Anthony Steele

illustrated by
Dario Brizuela

STONE ARCH BOOKS
a capstone imprint

←YOU CHOOSE→
SUPERMAN

Lex Luthor wants Metallo to be the newest hero of Metropolis. But when the cyborg menace breaks free of Luthor's control, he goes on the attack! Can the Man of Steel overpower Metallo before he gets his revenge? Only YOU can help stop him. With your help, the Man of Steel can defeat Metallo's deadly plans in *Metallo Attacks!*

Follow the directions at the bottom of each page. The choices YOU make will change the outcome of the story. After you finish one path, go back and read the others for more Superman adventures!

VROOOOM!

The sleek fighter jet zooms over the aircraft carrier. Jimmy Olsen raises his camera to take photographs of the fast aircraft. Clark Kent raises his pad and pencil to take notes. The two friends and coworkers are gathering information for a story for the *Daily Planet*.

"Look at that thing go, Mr. Kent," says Jimmy. "That jet is almost as fast as Superman!"

Clark chuckles and turns to his friend. "I don't know about that, Jimmy."

Clark and Jimmy stand among other reporters on the deck of the large Navy ship, *Elissa*. The group has gathered for this floating press conference at sea.

"This may look like an ordinary fighter jet," says Admiral Jenkins. "But you'll be surprised to know that the pilot is no longer in control."

The reporters gasp as the jet swings around and heads back toward them.

Turn the page.

"This fighter is flown by an artificial intelligence control unit developed by LexCorp," the admiral continues. "It can react one thousand times faster than the human body."

The jet cuts left and zips toward several floating targets. Its machine guns roar to life.

BRRAK-AK-AK-AK-AK-AK!

Bullets stream from the guns, shattering the targets into a million splinters. The jet fighter fires two missiles, and two more targets explode.

VOOM! KA-BOOOM!

The reporters aboard the ship applaud as the plane soars high into the sky.

"And that is just a small sample of what this new control unit can do," says the admiral. "Once it's been thoroughly tested, we'll no longer need to send pilots into battle."

The fighter jet reappears high above the aircraft carrier. Its engines roar as it dives toward the large ship. Admiral Jenkins squints up at the incoming plane.

"What is it doing?" asks the admiral.

BRRAK-AK-AK-AK-AK-AK!

The fighter jet opens fire! The crowd of reporters and crew members scatter as bullets strike the deck of the ship. Jimmy has his camera aimed up at the approaching plane. His camera clicks away as a stream of bullets heads toward him. Clark quickly grabs the back of Jimmy's collar and jerks him clear. The plane pulls up at the last second and buzzes over the ship.

"Thanks, Mr. Kent," says Jimmy. He runs over to the side of the ship to get more pictures.

"Tell the pilot to abort the test!" orders the admiral. "Get control of that jet right now!"

A sailor wearing a headset shrugs his shoulders. "She's been trying to, sir," the sailor replied. "The jet isn't responding. It's now locked on an attack course and headed for the coast . . . toward Metropolis."

Turn the page.

Clark has seen and heard enough. With everyone watching the runaway jet, he is able to slip out of the crowd. Clark runs to the other side of the ship and dives over the railing. But he doesn't splash into the ocean. With lightning speed, Clark Kent removes his suit and glasses to reveal the red and blue uniform beneath. The reporter from the *Daily Planet* is actually Superman — the Man of Steel!

Superman flies just above the ocean surface. Jets of water trail behind him as he races toward the fighter plane. He quickly catches up to it and flies up to the cockpit.

"Superman!" shouts the pilot. "Glad you're here. I can't stop this thing!"

"I'll take care of it," the Man of Steel assures her. "Can you eject?"

The pilot shakes her head and punches the glass covering her head. "The canopy is locked tight!"

Superman flies up and plants his feet on top of the jet. He reaches down and easily rips away the glass canopy.

"Thank you, Superman," says the pilot. She pushes a button, and her chair blasts out of the cockpit. Once clear, her parachute opens, and she safely drifts to the ocean surface.

Suddenly, the fighter jet turns on its side, flinging Superman free. Superman hovers in the air as the plane swings around in a wide arc. The jet straightens out and heads straight for the Man of Steel.

VRROOOOSH!

The jet nearly rams into Superman. But he is faster than a speeding bullet. Superman easily dodges away from the incoming plane.

Turn the page.

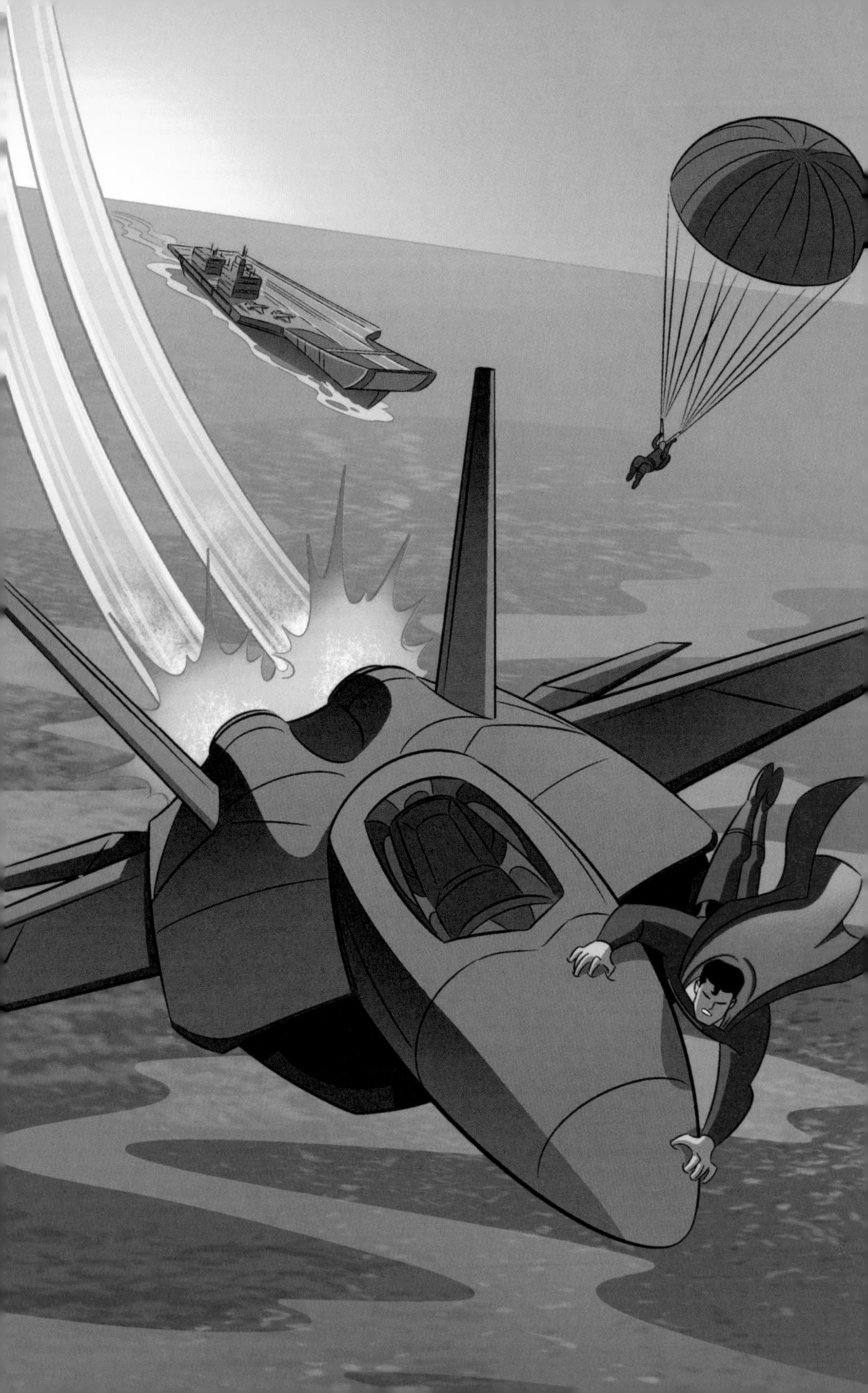

The jet zooms past him but swings around for another attack. Someone is obviously controlling the plane. It turns toward Superman and fires two missiles. The rockets zigzag toward the Man of Steel. Superman flies forward and catches the missiles, one in each hand. He squeezes them until they explode.

VOOM! KA-BOOOM!

When the smoke clears, Superman hovers in the same spot, dusting off his hands. The fighter jet buzzes by him, making his cape flap in the breeze. The jet continues on its course toward Metropolis.

"Oh no, you don't," says Superman. He takes off after the jet.

When Superman catches up to the jet, it's almost to the city. The tall skyscrapers loom closer and closer. The Man of Steel uses his X-ray vision to scan the inside of the plane. He quickly spots a long cylinder with *LexCorp* printed on the side. It's the control unit!

Turn the page.

Superman pokes his fingertips through the plane's metal body as if it were made of paper. He peels back the metal skin to expose the control unit. With his other hand, Superman reaches in and rips out the unit. The plane immediately drops from the air and splashes into the ocean.

Holding the cylinder in one hand, Superman dives into the water. He swims under the plane and lifts it out of the ocean. He then flies the plane back to the aircraft carrier and carefully sets it down on the ship's deck.

"Thank heavens you were here," says Admiral Jenkins. "We're picking up the pilot now. If that plane reached the city there's no telling how much damage it would've caused."

Superman hands the control unit to the admiral. "Although airplanes are still the safest way to travel, I would only trust a human pilot to fly one."

"I agree," says the admiral. He runs his fingers over the LexCorp logo. "We'll see what Lex Luthor has to say about this."

"Have a good day, Admiral," says Superman as he flies into the sky. Jimmy Olsen and the other reporters push in to get a closer look at the faulty plane. Jimmy zooms his camera in on the LexCorp control unit. "This'll make a great story, huh, Mr. Kent?" He glances around. Clark Kent isn't with the rest of the reporters.

Jimmy doesn't notice that Superman has zipped back to the other side of the ship. The Man of Steel grabs his stashed suit and glasses and quickly changes back into his secret identity: Clark Kent. Once dressed, Clark returns to join the others.

"Hey, where were you, Mr. Kent?" asks Jimmy.

"Sorry, Jimmy," says Clark. He rubs his stomach. "I got a little seasick. What did I miss?"

"Oh, not much. Only Superman bringing in that runaway jet!" exclaims Jimmy. "I don't think the artificial intelligence control unit was a success."

Turn the page.

"Yes," agrees Clark. "It sounds as if Lex Luthor has some questions to answer about his faulty equipment."

"Isn't Ms. Lane covering his press conference this afternoon?" asks Jimmy.

"I think you're right," replies Clark. "Let's join her and get some answers of our own."

Later that day, Clark and Jimmy join the crowd of reporters gathered in front of the tall LexCorp building. They stroll up to meet fellow *Daily Planet* reporter, Lois Lane.

"What are you two doing here?" asks Lois. "Aren't you supposed to be floating out in the ocean somewhere?"

Clark and Jimmy explain the morning's mayhem and how Superman flew to the rescue. "I'd like to get a statement from Luthor about his faulty equipment," Clark adds.

"Slow down there, Smallville," says Lois. She enjoys using Clark's tiny hometown as his nickname. "This is my assignment, so I get to go first."

Soon, the press conference begins, and Lex Luthor steps onto the large stage. Jimmy, along with the other photographers, takes pictures of the sharply-dressed, bald billionaire.

"Welcome, ladies and gentlemen of the press," says Lex Luthor. "For too long Metropolis has relied on an alien from another planet to be its protector."

"Not this again," whispers Lois. "Luthor has never been a fan of Superman."

"Maybe that's because there has never been a different choice," Luthor continues. "Well, that changes today."

Luthor points to the sky, and a metallic figure drops into view. Fire blasts from the bottom of its feet as it nears the stage. The crowd gasps as the rockets cut off and the robot drops to the stage with a loud THUD! Everyone recognizes the robotic villain.

"Holy macaroni," exclaims Jimmy with a gasp. "That's Metallo!"

Turn the page.

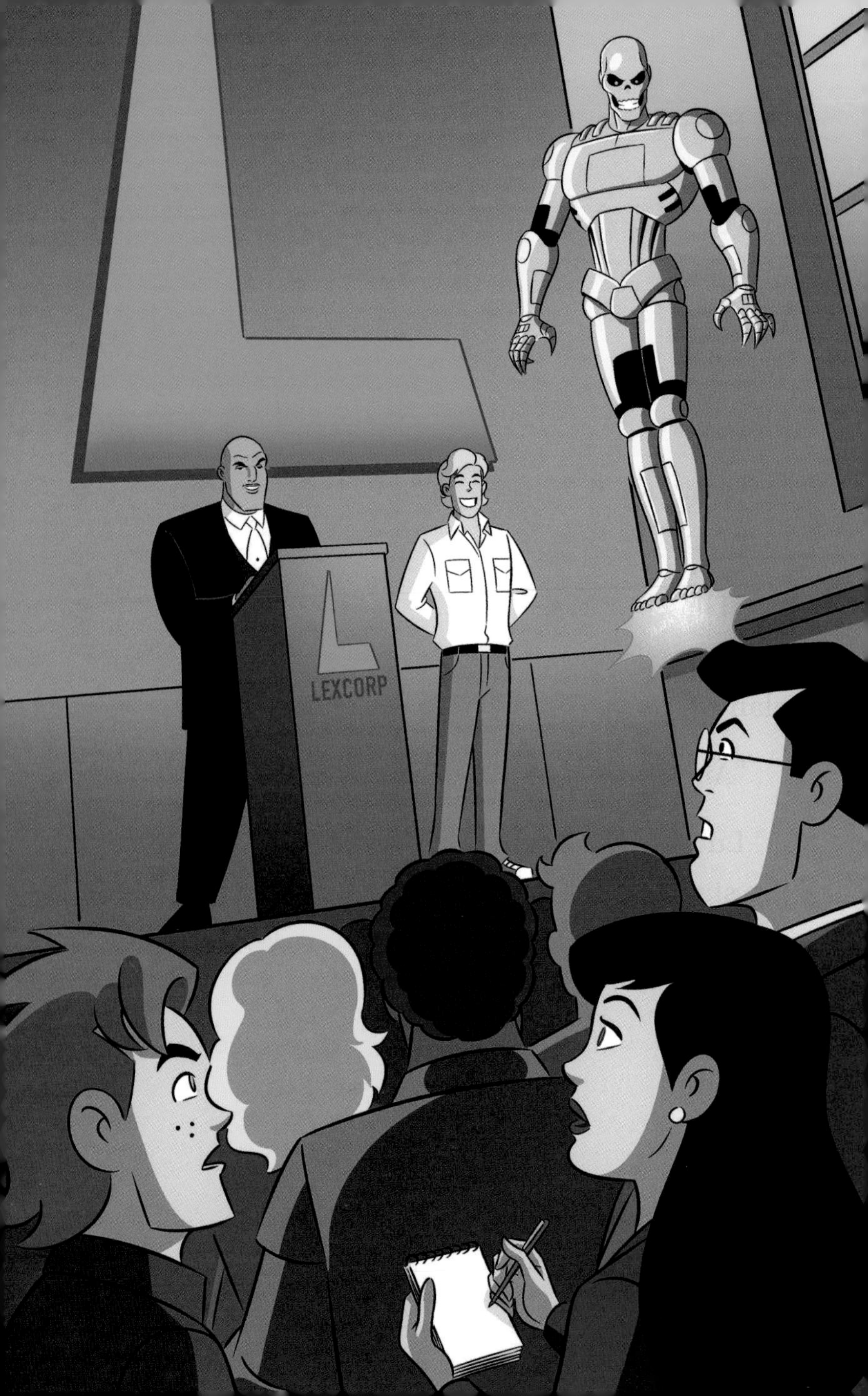
LEXCORP

Luthor raises both hands. "Settle down, everyone. You're perfectly safe, I assure you." The crowd's murmur fades, and Luthor continues his speech. "Many know this as simply Metallo. But I know him as John Corben. This man had a deadly disease. But I was able to save him by placing his brain inside a cyborg body."

"I thought Corben wanted revenge against you for trapping him in that robotic body," says Lois.

"That's all in the past, Ms. Lane," replies Luthor. "With the help of my newest researcher, I plan to make Corben human again."

"And just who would that be?" asks Lois.

Luthor gestures to a young man on the side of the stage. "Josh Bear," says Luthor. "He's almost as bright as I was at his age." The blond man smiles and waves to the reporters.

Turn the page.

"In the meantime, as Metallo, John Corben has vowed to protect Metropolis as only a true hero should," says Luthor.

Metallo steps forward. "I will protect Metropolis," he says in an electronic voice. "I will protect everyone."

The cyborg crouches and leaps into the air. Flames erupt from the bottoms of his feet, and he soars high above the crowd. The metal man flies into the city and disappears around a nearby skyscraper.

"We no longer need Superman to protect us," says Luthor. "Now we have Metallo. And me, of course."

Lex Luthor spins on his heels and marches toward the LexCorp building. Reporters try to ask him questions, but he disappears inside without saying another word.

"Well, how do you like that?" asks Lois. "He's got some nerve dropping that bombshell on us. And then he just leaves!"

"I think there's more to this story than meets the eye," says Clark.

"You can say that again," agrees Lois. "And I'm going to find out what it is."

If Superman trails after Metallo, turn to page 22.
If Clark Kent investigates Josh Bear, turn to page 36.
If Clark sticks with Lois and Jimmy, turn to page 45.

"Well, I better get back to the office and write up the fighter jet story," Clark says, putting away his pad and pencil.

"You do that, Smallville," says Lois. She looks over the crowd toward the LexCorp building. "I'm going to see what else I can get out of Luthor."

Clark walks away from the crowded sidewalk and ducks into a nearby alley. When he's sure no one is looking, he quickly transforms into Superman and takes to the sky in search of Metallo.

Superman doesn't like the idea of the cyborg flying around unchecked. In the past, Metallo was one of his greatest enemies. It's difficult to believe that the metal maniac would choose to help the people of Metropolis.

Superman uses his super-hearing and vision to scan the city. He can hear a cricket chirp in the park and see through entire city blocks with his X-ray vision. But he doesn't find any sign of Metallo. Metropolis is a very big city.

Suddenly, a familiar sound screams out at him — police sirens. Superman pours on the speed, flying toward the source of the commotion. He zips around skyscrapers and past bridges until he spots trouble at the edge of town. Four police cruisers are chasing an armored truck down a busy street. His X-ray vision reveals three masked men inside a truck full of money.

"This should be quick," says Superman. "I'll stop these crooks and then finish my search for —"

Metallo flies past Superman. The metal man zips by so fast that the Man of Steel tumbles through the air in his wake. "I will protect Metropolis," Metallo says in a robotic voice. "I will protect everyone."

The metal man lands directly in front of the armored vehicle. The truck honks its horn and tries to swerve, but it's too late.

Turn the page.

CRASH!!!

The truck slams into Metallo. The cyborg doesn't budge, and the front of the vehicle crumples around him. Two of the crooks crash through the windshield and tumble to a stop on the street next to the metal man.

"Those men deserve to go to jail, not the hospital," Superman says to himself. He flies down to the scene.

As the police cars pull to a stop behind the wrecked truck, Metallo leaps onto its roof. He peels back the metal roof and reaches in to grab the third crook.

"Please don't hurt me," pleads the masked man.

BAM! Superman slams into Metallo, knocking him from the roof.

"Back off, Metallo," says Superman. He holds the robot in a bear hug. "You could have seriously hurt someone."

"I will protect Metropolis," says Metallo. "I will protect everyone."

The cyborg breaks free from Superman's grasp. Then he backhands the Man of Steel. Superman flies backward and slams into a building. The cement wall cracks on impact.

Metallo's head turns toward the armored truck. One of the crooks slips past the police officers and runs into a nearby scrapyard. The cyborg flies after him.

Superman is dazed from Metallo's attack. He stands up and shakes his head to clear his mind. "I almost forgot how hard Metallo can hit," he mutters to himself. Superman takes to the air and follows the cyborg. "I can't let him get his metal hands on anyone else."

Metallo flies past rows of junked cars and piles of scrap metal. He searches the junkyard for the escaped criminal. He finally spots the masked man climbing into the control cab of a large crane. The cyborg moves in, but his path is soon blocked — by the Man of Steel.

Turn the page.

"Stand down, Corben," says Superman. "I won't let you hurt anyone else."

"I will protect Metropolis," repeats Metallo. "I will protect everyone."

"Why do you keep saying that?" asks Superman.

"Ruin our big score, will ya?" asks a voice behind Superman. It's the crook from the armored car. The masked man sits at the crane's controls.

Superman ducks just in time as a large metal disk swings by. The crook flicks a switch and the disk begins to hum. The powerful electromagnet comes to life.

KLANG! Metallo's body slams into the magnet.

POP! TZZZ! TZZZZ!!

Sparks fly and electricity crackles all over Metallo's body. "I will protect . . ." Metallo tries to say. "I . . . will . . . protect . . ."

"That magnet is hurting him somehow," says Superman. He aims his heat vision at the crane's control panel. Two red beams shoot from his eyes.

"Yikes!" shouts the crook as the panel overheats. The masked man scrambles out of the cab and takes off into the junkyard.

With the magnet shut off, Metallo falls to the ground. "I . . . I . . . I . . ." he repeats in his electronic voice.

Superman lands next to him. "Corben? Are you all right?"

"I . . . I . . . I'm free!" Metallo shouts. He flies into the air. "That magnet shorted out Lex Luthor's control over me." He glares down at Superman. "Now, I will have my revenge!"

If Superman confronts Metallo in the scrapyard,
turn to page 28.

If Superman draws Metallo away from the city,
turn to page 53.

"There's no need for revenge," Superman tells him. "If Luthor has wronged you, I'll guarantee he'll get what's coming to him."

"You can't guarantee that," Metallo replies. "Luthor's wealth buys him out of any trouble."

Metallo ignites his jets and takes to the air. Superman zips in front of him, blocking his way. "I'm afraid I can't let you do that."

"Are you forgetting what Luthor gave me to power this body?" Metallo asks. A panel in his chest slides open, revealing a glowing green rock.

"Ugh!" Superman winces in pain. "Kryptonite." The Man of Steel slowly floats to the ground. The radiation from the rock saps away his powers.

Metallo hovers above Superman triumphantly. "Stay out of this, Superman." He turns to fly away.

Weak and unable to fly himself, Superman grabs a scrapped car door and hurls it with all his might. He sends it flying toward the cyborg.

WHAK!

It smashes against Metallo, knocking him into a pile of junk.

With Metallo's Kryptonite heart far enough away, Superman staggers to his feet. "I have to find a way to fight him and stay away from that Kryptonite."

"Are you really that foolish to pick a fight with me here, of all places?" asks Metallo.

Suddenly, the entire mound of scrap metal seems to come to life. Junked cars, rusted metal beams, old appliances, and miles of wiring swirl together. Soon, the mountain of metal forms into a giant version of Metallo. The enormous robot stares down at Superman with glowing green eyes.

"It's time to squash you like the bug you are," Metallo says with an electronic laugh.

Turn the page.

The massive mechanical man raises a giant foot and slams it toward Superman. The Man of Steel barely leaps to safety as the foot smashes the ground.

Superman takes to the air and flies toward the metallic monster. He balls his fist, ready to shatter the giant trash-heap robot with one punch. Unfortunately, the green glow of Kryptonite shines from inside the robot's chest.

Superman grunts as the radiation hits him. But that's not all that hits him. Metallo's giant hand swats him while he's distracted.

SMACK!

The super hero slams into the base of another junk pile. Old cars and scrap metal topple over and bury the Man of Steel.

"You can't hide from me," Metallo taunts. He bends down and digs through the pile of metal. "Come out, come out, wherever you are!"

Metallo lifts up a smashed truck and looks beneath it. Superman isn't there. Metallo doesn't see that the Man of Steel is holding on to the underside of the truck, hiding from the enormous robot.

I have to find a way to defeat this metal maniac, Superman thinks.

If Superman scans the area for something useful, turn to page 32.

If Superman lures Metallo into a trap, turn to page 65.

Superman is weakened by the Kryptonite, but he can still use his X-ray vision. He scans the surrounding junk piles for anything he can use. He sees a large rectangular object. It's the only thing in the junkyard that he can't see through. That means that it must be made of lead!

"Lead blocks my X-ray vision," he says to himself. "But it can also block the radiation from Metallo's Kryptonite heart."

Superman leaps from his hiding place and dives into the junk pile. Scraps fly as he moves through the metal as easily as a fish swims through water.

Metallo drops the truck and reaches after him. "You can't escape me, Superman!" The robot touches the pile of metal, and the loose scraps begin sticking to his hand. "I am truly in my element." Metallo's new body grows bigger as he absorbs the metal around him.

Superman manages to grab the lead plate just as he is swept up into the surging mass of metal.

Holding the plate like a shield, he turns the lead plate to block the deadly Kryptonite radiation. "Much better," he says as he pushes his way free from Metallo's enormous arm.

As he frees himself, Superman grabs a large chain with his free hand. He explodes from Metallo's arm with a shield in one hand and an old wrecking ball dangling from the other.

"Get back here!" Metallo shouts as he tries to snatch Superman out of the air.

Superman dodges the attack and swings the wrecking ball. It smashes into Metallo's hand, scattering the scrap metal. The trash-heap robot reaches out with his other hand, but Superman smashes that one too.

However, Metallo is far from being helpless. His hand reforms as more metal is sucked up toward him. The robotic man laughs wickedly as he grows taller and taller. The surrounding mountains of metal shrink as they are absorbed into Metallo's new body.

Turn the page.

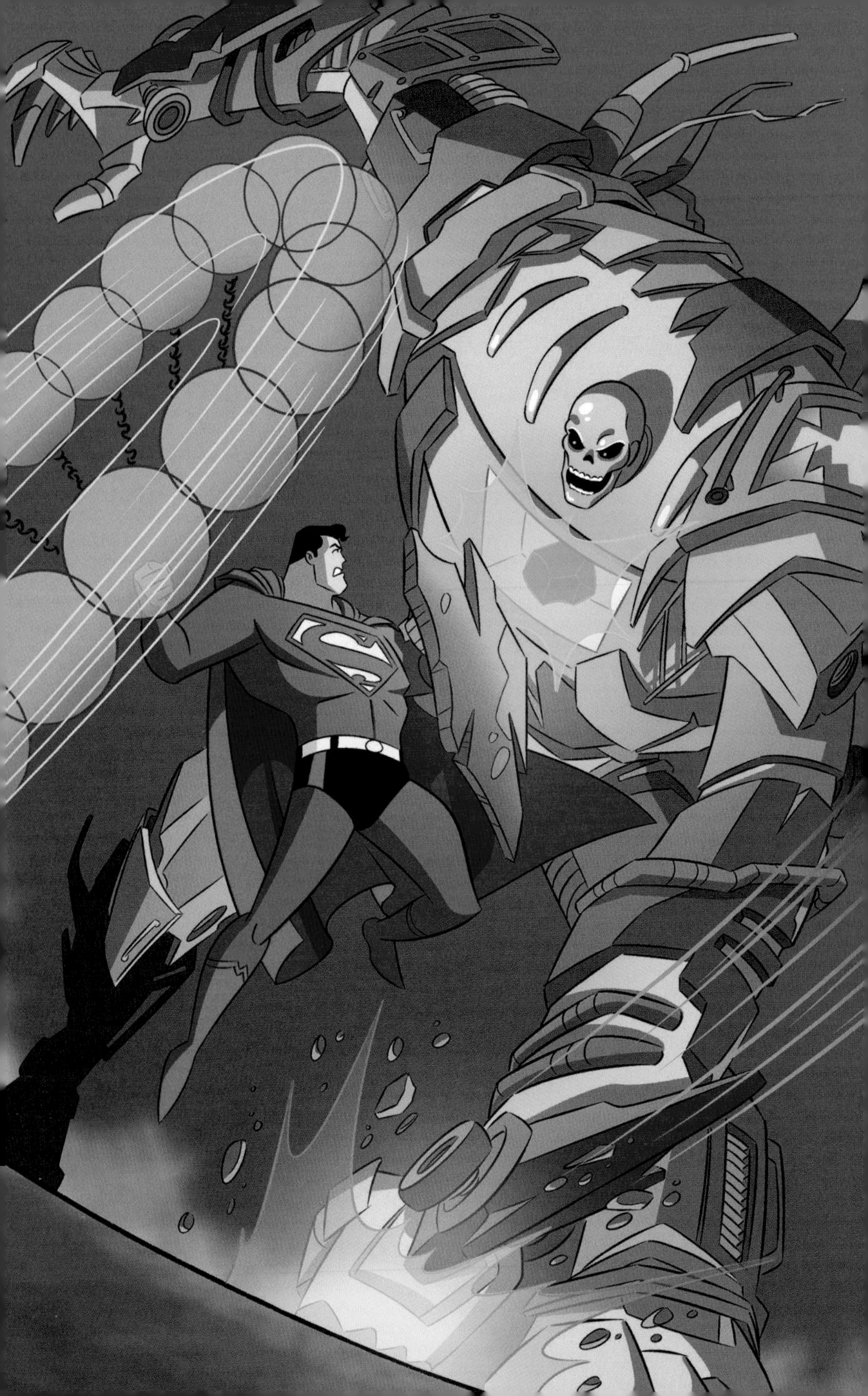

"I have to stop him before he absorbs every piece of metal in Metropolis," says Superman. "But I'm powerless without this shield."

The Man of Steel scans the area once more. A glint of light catches his eyes. A shiny, polished hubcap stands out among the heaps of rusted metal. This gives Superman an idea.

Superman floats closer to the hubcap. While protecting himself with his lead shield, he blasts the hubcap with his heat vision. Two thin red beams hit the hubcap and bounce off. They angle up to Metallo's chest and strike the green rock embedded there. The Kryptonite turns red and then explodes into dust.

"No!" Metallo shouts. His giant body falls apart around him. He falls to the ground, buried beneath the rest of the useless metal.

Superman drops his weapons and flies down to the pile of junk. "Don't worry, Corben," he says. "When they pull you out of this scrap heap, I'll make sure you aren't recycled."

THE END

To follow another path, turn to page 21.

After the press conference, Clark is surprised to see Josh Bear get into a taxi. Clark expected Bear to work in the LexCorp building with Lex Luthor. Clark catches another cab and has the driver follow him. To his surprise, Bear's cab pulls to a stop in front of another large office building. The sign above it reads: *Grizzly Games*. Bear hops out of the cab and goes inside.

Clark pays for his own cab and enters the building. A young receptionist sits behind the desk in the main entry.

"May I help you?" she asks.

"Clark Kent from the *Daily Planet* to see Josh Bear," Clark replies.

After a short wait, Josh Bear exits a door behind the receptionist.

"I hope you don't mind, Mr. Bear," says Clark. "But I wanted to ask you some follow-up questions after that unusual press conference today."

"Not at all," says Bear. "And call me Josh." He gives Clark a fist bump. "Let me give you the grand tour."

Josh leads Clark out of the entryway and into a room full of people working on computers. At least, that's what it looks like at first glance. But when Clark looks closer, he sees that they're all playing different kinds of video games.

"*Grizzly Games* . . ." says Clark. "So, you make video games?"

"That's right," replies Josh.

"Why would Lex Luthor hire a game developer to work against Superman?" asks Clark.

Josh comes to a halt. "Wait. *Against* Superman?" asks Josh. "Man, I wouldn't work against Superman. I only want to help him. Heck, I'm his biggest fan!"

Clark smiles. "Well, it's well known that Lex Luthor isn't Superman's biggest fan. And if you're working with Lex . . ."

Turn the page.

Josh marches toward a closed door. "Look, I'll prove it. This is my office." Josh opens the door to reveal a room full of Superman souvenirs. Superman posters cover the walls. The desk holds Superman action figures, a Superman mouse pad, and a Man of Steel coffee mug. Josh even unbuttons his shirt to reveal a Superman T-shirt underneath.

Clark holds up both hands. "Okay, okay. You've convinced me," he says with a laugh. "But what does Lex Luthor need with a game developer?"

Josh grins. "Because I've taken virtual reality to the next level." He points to a futuristic chair. Black gloves sit on the armrests, and a large helmet is suspended over the top.

"I'm still not sure what this has to do with Lex Luthor," says Clark.

"You should give it a try and find out," Josh suggests.

If Clark tries the virtual reality game, turn to page 40.
If Clark wants more information first, turn to page 59.

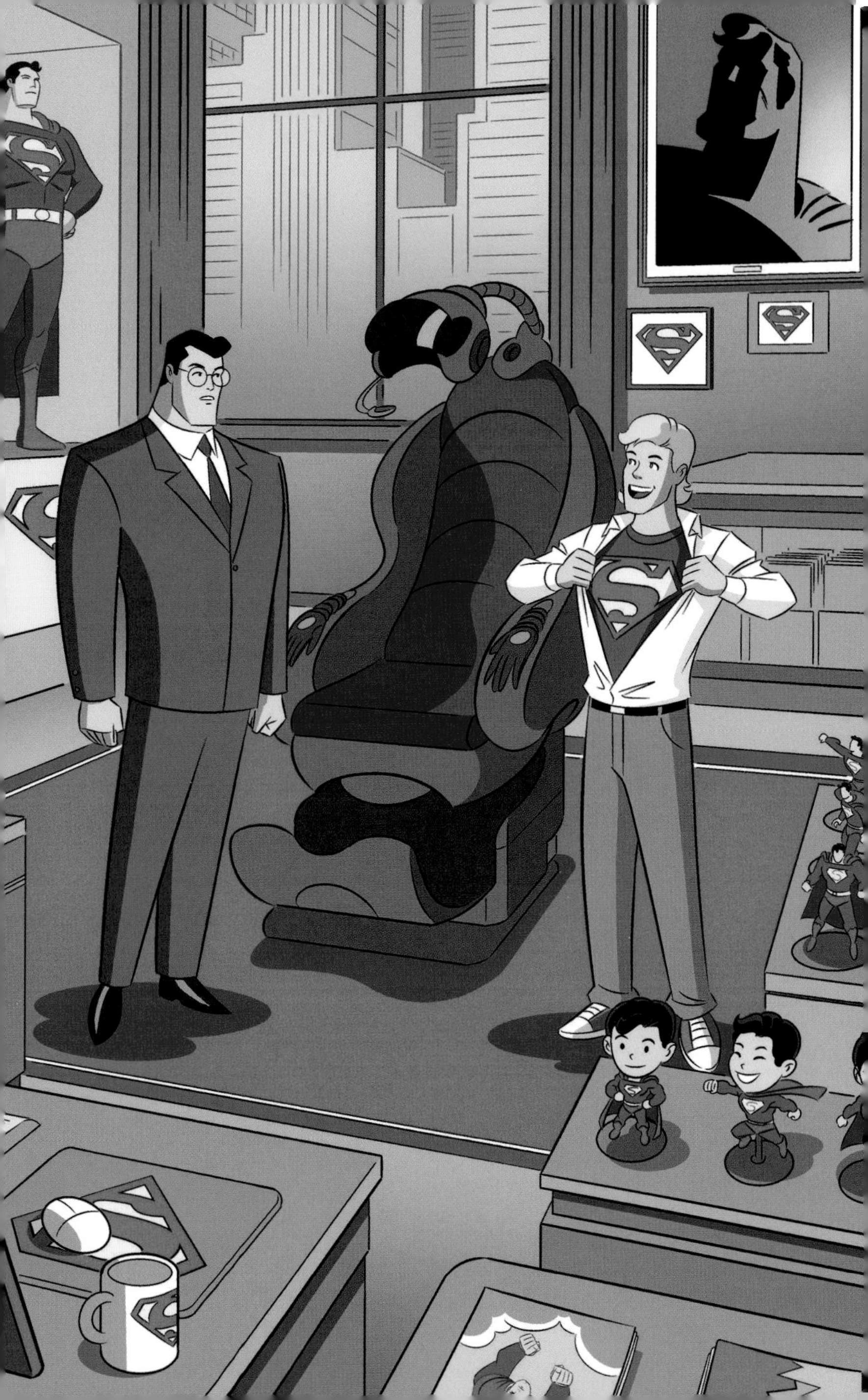

"All right," says Clark. "How do I do it?"

"Just have a seat. I'll hook you up," says Josh.

Clark sits in the chair while Josh helps him put on the gloves. When they're in place, the young man places the helmet on Clark's head. After strapping it on, Josh lowers the visor over the reporter's eyes.

KA-BLAM!

No sooner had the visor been lowered than an explosion rocks the room. Superman posters and figurines scatter everywhere, and a big hole appears in the wall. A metallic figure steps through the hole — it's Metallo!

"I found you, Superman," the figure announces in an electronic voice. "Prepare to meet your doom!"

The cyborg snatches Clark Kent out of the chair and jerks him back out through the hole in the wall. Clark soars high into the sky. When he looks down, he sees that he's already changed into Superman.

"All right, Metallo," says Superman. "It's time to shut you down permanently."

Superman flies back toward Grizzly Games only to see Metallo racing up to meet him. The Man of Steel jerks to one side just as the cyborg throws a punch. Metallo misses and circles back for another attack.

I've battled Metallo enough to know that his metal body can take a hit, Superman thinks. *I won't have to hold back.*

Superman balls his hands together into a double fist and swings at the attacking cyborg.

SMACK!

The robot tumbles back through the air. The Man of Steel doesn't give Metallo a chance to recover. He catches up to him and delivers three mighty blows in a row.

POW! SMASH! CRUNCH!

That's when Superman notices something very strange. A long rectangle with Metallo's face floats in the sky above the cyborg.

Turn the page.

As the Man of Steel is distracted, Metallo spins around and punches Superman in the jaw.

BAM! Superman flies backward. That's when he notices a second rectangle, showing his own face, floating above him.

The super hero doesn't have time to think about the strange floating objects. Metallo rockets toward him. The metal man makes a fist and slams it into Superman's stomach.

OOF! As Superman tumbles backward, he sees that the object above him is now shorter.

Metallo swoops in for another attack, but Superman is ready for him. The Man of Steel blocks a punch and then a kick. Superman counters with two punches of his own.

BAP! KAPOW! He sends the cyborg flying end over end. Superman sees the first rectangle has shrunk even more than the one above him.

Superman squints and blasts Metallo with his heat vision. The Metallo's rectangle gets shorter and shorter.

Turn to page 44.

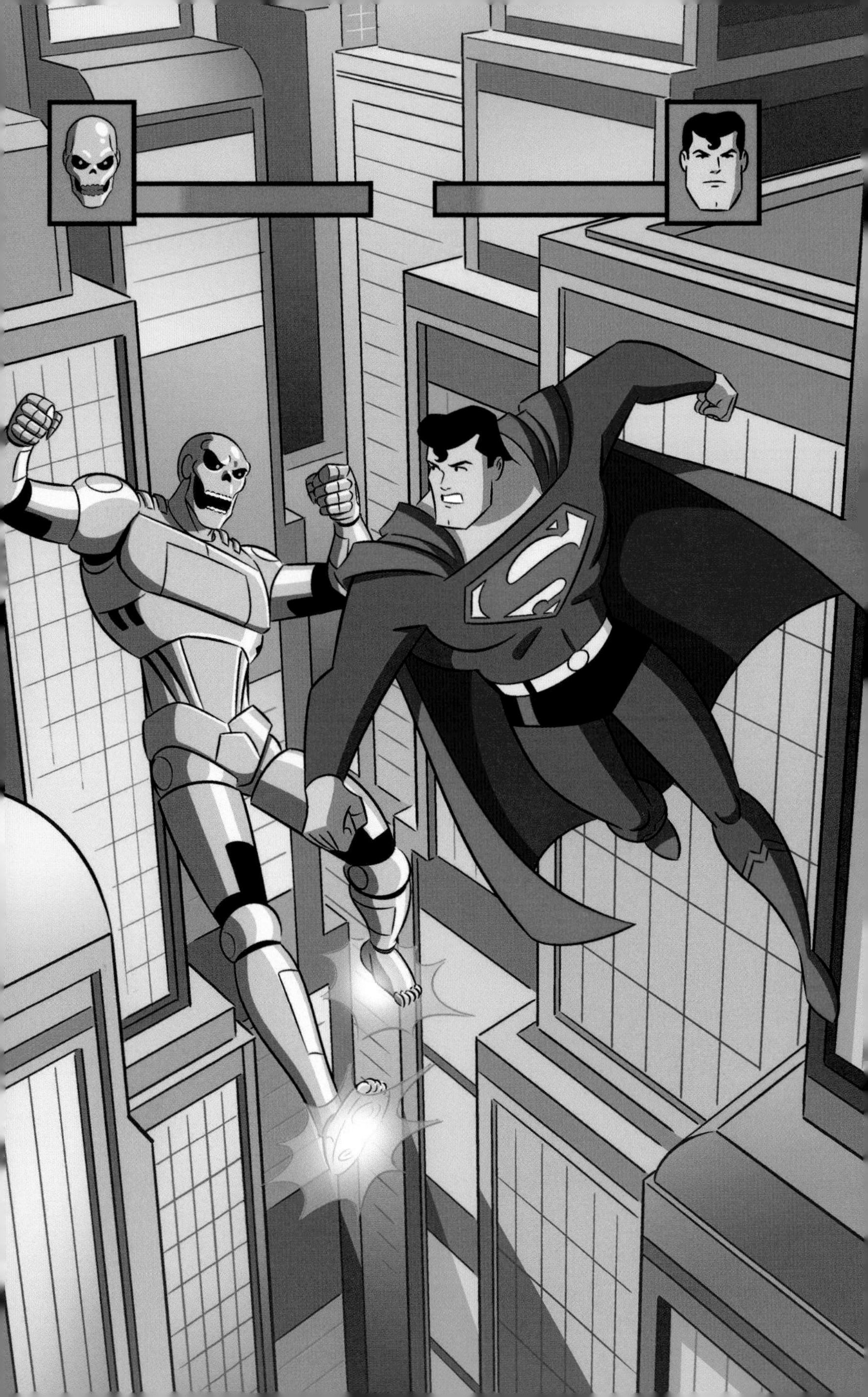

"Aarrgghh!" the cyborg yells in his electronic robotic voice.

Superman balls a fist and hurtles toward his stunned foe. With all his might, the super hero punches the metallic villain. Metallo tumbles backward, and his rectangle disappears completely.

WHOOSH!

After a flash of blinding light, Clark Kent slowly removes the visor from his head.

"What did you think?" asks Josh Bear.

"Wow," Clark says, blinking his eyes. "It felt like I really was Superman."

"I know, right?" says Josh.

Clark raises an eyebrow. "So what's the Lex Luthor connection?"

Josh rolls his eyes. "Mr. Luthor likes to stop by here and pretend to be Superman."

Clark chuckles. "That's going to make a great story for the *Daily Planet.*"

THE END

To follow another path, turn to page 21.

Clark eyes Lois suspiciously. "What are you up to, Lois?"

"Wrong question," Lois replies as she drapes her arms over Clark and Jimmy's shoulders. "The right question is: what are *we* up to?"

"I don't like the sound of this, Ms. Lane," Jimmy says nervously.

"Oh, be a sport, Jimmy," Lois says, rolling her eyes. "I just need to get past those LexCorp guards and get upstairs to ask Luthor some questions."

"But won't Mr. Luthor just call the guards up and kick you out?" asks Jimmy.

Lois smiles. "Eventually. But Luthor likes the sound of his own voice too much. I bet he'll answer a couple of questions first."

"Happy to help, Lois," Clark says. He turns to Jimmy. "Just get your camera ready and follow my lead."

Turn the page.

When Lois gets in position farther down the sidewalk, Clark and Jimmy march up to the two security guards in front of the building.

"Excuse me? Gentlemen?" says Clark. "I'm Clark Kent from the *Daily Planet*."

The taller guard holds out a hand. "No reporters get in," he says. "Mr. Luthor's orders."

Clark laughs. "Oh, I don't want in. I want to talk to you two."

"Us?" asks the shorter guard. "Why's that?"

"I'm writing a story about . . ." Clark says, waving a hand dramatically, ". . . those who guard greatness."

The guards look at each other with confusion and then back at Clark Kent. "Really?" asks the taller guard.

Clark nods. "Oh, yeah. I'm speaking to LexCorp guards, Wayne Industries guards, and so on . . ." He pulls a pad and pencil out of his pocket. "So, how does Lex Luthor treat you guys?"

"Not too bad, I guess," the tall guard says as he rubs his chin.

"Good pay?" Clark asks. "Nice benefits?"

"We do all right," replies the short guard.

"Say, how about we get a shot of these two?" Clark asks Jimmy. "Right under the LexCorp logo."

"Uh, okay," replies Jimmy.

Clark gets between the men and ushers them toward the sidewalk. Once in position, he steps away to get a better look. Jimmy raises his camera and photographs the men. The bright camera flash makes them blink several times.

With their backs turned, the guards don't see Lois sneak into the LexCorp building. Once she's out of sight, Clark turns back to Jimmy. "That looks wonderful. Maybe even front page material."

"Front page?" asks the shorter guard. "Really?"

Clark gives them a wink. "Keep an eye out for it." Clark puts a hand on Jimmy's shoulder and steers him down the sidewalk.

Turn the page.

"I can't believe that worked, Mr. Kent," Jimmy says as he wipes the sweat from his brow.

"We better not be here when Luthor calls for those guards to get rid of Lois," Clark says. "I'll meet you back at the office."

"Okay, Mr. Kent." Jimmy hails a taxi and heads back to the *Daily Planet*.

With Jimmy gone and Lois on her way to see Lex Luthor, Clark Kent ducks into a parked delivery van. He exits the other side as Superman. Without anyone seeing him, he flies up toward the top of the LexCorp building.

Meanwhile, Lois Lane steps out of the elevator onto the top floor. She marches across the large office toward the huge glass desk and the bald man sitting behind it.

"Care to explain how a super-villain is supposed to be a super hero for Metropolis?" she asks.

Lex Luthor sighs. "Ms. Lane. Why am I not surprised?"

He presses a red button on his desk before standing. "I have time to answer your one question before my security guards escort you out of the building."

"Good," says Superman as he hovers over Luthor's office balcony. "Because I'd like to hear the answer to this one too." He lands and walks into the office.

Luthor points to Superman. "There! There is your answer, Ms. Lane. Because even though Metallo is mostly metal, he is still John Corben, human." He snarls at the Man of Steel. "Our so-called all-powerful protector isn't even from this planet. The last surviving alien from a dying world . . . or so he tells us."

"But Metallo is evil," says Lois. "How can you even imagine him to be a hero?"

"I don't have to imagine, Ms. Lane," Luthor replies as he gives his smartwatch a few taps. Just then, Metallo rockets into view. He flies into the office and lands next to Superman.

Turn the page.

"You're controlling him?" asks Superman.

Luthor shrugs. "Look, I told Corben I'd help find a way to get him back into a regular body. And I will. But in the meantime, why have all this power go to waste?"

DING!

The elevator opens, and the two security guards step out. They take in the scene with wide eyes.

"Uh, Mr. Luthor?" says the short guard. "Don't get the wrong idea. We're happy to escort the lady out of the building . . . but how do we handle Superman?"

"Don't worry about it," Luthor says with a wave of his hand. "I suppose a demonstration is in order anyway."

He taps his watch again, and Metallo swings his arm to punch Superman. Taken by surprise, the Man of Steel flies back and smashes into Lex's desk.

KRASH! It shatters beneath him.

"That was a ten-thousand dollar desk," Luthor says with a smirk. "No matter. It was worth it."

"Stop it!" Lois shouts. She runs forward and grabs for Luthor's wrist.

Luthor jerks away his arm and snaps his fingers. "Hold her," he orders. The two guards rush forward and take hold of the struggling reporter.

Meanwhile, Superman gets to his feet. "You'll pay for that, Lex."

"I think not," Luthor says with a chuckle. "Remember what I used to power Metallo's body?" Luthor taps his watch, and the hatch on the cyborg's chest opens. A glowing green rock is mounted there. It is Metallo's source of power.

"Ugh!" Superman stumbles as he is bathed in green light.

"Kryptonite," says Luthor. "A piece of your home planet. The only thing that weakens you, hurts you, and makes you just like the rest of us."

Turn the page.

"Stop it!" Lois shouts again. She can't break free from the guards. "You're hurting him."

Luthor laughs. "Oh, I haven't even begun to hurt him." He taps his watch a few more times, and Metallo springs into action.

SMACK! The cyborg backhands Superman, sending him sailing across the room.

The robot marches after him and grabs the hero's cape. He whips Superman into the air and then slams him back onto the floor. **BAM!**

Superman can't fight back. The deadly radiation saps his powers, making him weaker and weaker. He concentrates everything on his heat vision. He has just enough power for a single blast.

If Superman targets Lex Luthor, turn to page 55.
If he targets the floor, turn to page 69.

Metallo rockets toward Superman. The Man of Steel leaps into the air, dodging the attack. The cyborg slams into the ground, creating a huge crater.

"I have to get him out of the city," Superman says to himself. The super hero soars high into the sky.

Metallo flies after him. "It's not like you to run away from a fight, Superman," the cyborg says with a sneer.

Superman pours on the speed, leading the chase away from the city and over the harbor. Metallo slowly closes the gap between them. When they are far enough from the public, Superman turns to face his foe.

"This should be far enough," says Superman.

POW!

Superman punches the cyborg so hard that his metallic body skips across the water like a stone. The metal man makes ten skips before slamming into a large metal buoy.

Turn the page.

Metallo shakes his metal head before igniting his rockets. He rises into the air and grabs the tip of the buoy. He pulls it out of the water, ripping the metal frame away from its floating base.

As Metallo nears Superman, his chest opens to reveal his Kryptonite heart. Superman feels weak as the green radiation washes over him.

"I can't have you following me while I seek my revenge," Metallo says, wrapping the steel frame around Superman's weakened body. Then the cyborg drops Superman into the water.

SPLASH!

The Man of Steel sinks like a rock to the bottom of the ocean.

Being away from the Kryptonite, Superman begins to regain his strength. He snaps the metal straps and flies out of the water. He scans the area, but he's completely alone.

"Metallo got away," he says. "But I'll find him soon enough."

THE END

To follow another path, turn to page 21.

Using his heat vision, Superman aims a thin red beam at Luthor's watch. The device sparks and turns red with the heat.

"Agh!" Luthor shouts as he fumbles for the watch strap. He unhooks it, and the damaged device falls to the floor.

"What is this?" asks an electronic voice. Metallo examines his hands and glances around. "Luthor? He was controlling me?" He closes the hatch on his chest and marches toward Lex.

Luthor backs away. "Now, Corben . . . wait just a minute . . ." He looks back toward the men holding Lois. "Guards!"

But Lois is standing by herself.

DING! The elevator doors close with the guards inside.

With the Kryptonite sealed, Superman regains some strength. He tries to stand but stumbles. "Metallo . . . wait."

Turn the page.

"No one controls me!" Metallo shouts as he grabs Luthor by the shoulders. The cyborg's rockets ignite, and he rises into the air. Luthor's feet dangle off the ground as Metallo moves toward the balcony.

"Corben, listen to me. You can't hurt me," Luthor pleads. "I'm . . . I'm the one that's going to get you a human body, remember?"

"Yes, I can tell you're devoting every waking moment to the project," Metallo replies sarcastically. The cyborg then carries Luthor past the balcony and high into the air.

Superman weakly stands up and shuffles onto the balcony. "Come back, Corben," Superman says, leaning on the railing. "We can talk about this. Just let Luthor go."

"Oh, I plan to do just that," says Metallo. He laughs and releases his grip on Lex Luthor. The man falls as the cyborg flies away.

"I was afraid of that," Superman says as he dives over the railing.

Turn to page 58.

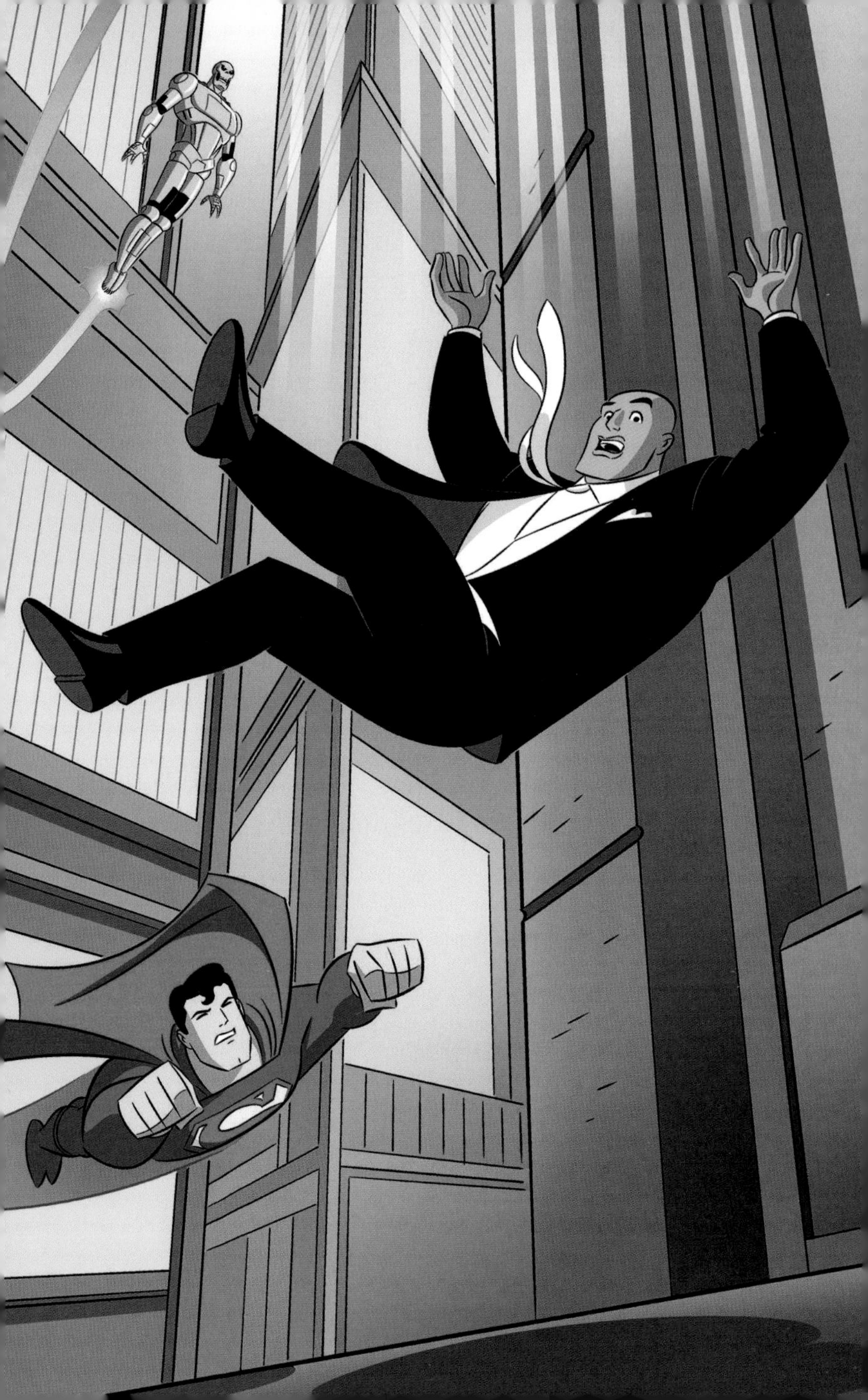

"Superman!" shouts Luthor. "Save me!"

The super hero flies toward the falling man. Still weak from the Kryptonite, it takes him longer than expected to catch up. Superman finally latches onto Luthor and pulls up at the last second. Superman groans as it takes every ounce of strength he has to stop their fall. He finally pulls to a stop just a few feet from the hard sidewalk.

"Don't need an alien to save you, huh?" Superman asks, setting Luthor gently on the ground.

Luthor straightens his tie. "This isn't over," he says as he marches back into the LexCorp building.

Superman scans the sky, looking for Metallo. The cyborg is gone, for now. "You're right, Lex. This isn't over at all," Superman says to himself.

THE END

To follow another path, turn to page 21.

"Maybe later," Clark replies. "Right now, I'd love to see more of your facility."

"You bet," says Josh. "Follow me."

The younger man leads Clark down a hallway and into a small, dark room. Inside, another man sits in front of a large computer screen. The man wears a futuristic helmet and gloves. As he moves his hands, two metal hands on the monitor move along with them. The player appears to be playing a game where he flies around a city like Metropolis.

"Is he testing one of your new games?" Clark asks the young game designer.

"Well, yes and no," Josh replies. "You were at the press conference today. Do you recognize the hands on the screen?"

Clark leans in for a closer look. The hands on the screen look silver and robotic. They look just like those belonging to . . .

"Metallo?" asks Clark.

Turn the page.

"That's right," says Josh. He pats the player on the shoulder. "This guy is actually piloting the Metallo you saw today."

Clark watches the screen and sees Metallo's view of the city. The metal robot zips past buildings while keeping up with a police chase on the street below. Several patrol cars chase an armored truck.

"Isn't it amazing?" asks Josh. "Now Superman doesn't have to do it all alone. Our Metallo can help deal with all the little stuff." Something on the computer monitor catches his eye. "Ooh, check this out."

Clark watches the screen as Metallo passes the armored truck and lands in the street in front of it. The truck tries to swerve but doesn't make it. The truck's grill fills the computer screen before it crashes directly into Metallo. The metal man doesn't move as two masked men crash through the windshield and fly past him.

"Amazing!" Josh says with a laugh.

I have to get out of here somehow, thinks Clark. *I have to stop that remote-controlled Metallo before he hurts someone.*

While Josh's eyes are glued to the screen, Clark moves to a nearby door. Hopefully he can sneak out while Josh watches the screen.

Clark opens the door and spots row upon row of computer bays inside a huge room. Each computer bay has a gamer sitting inside operating a virtual reality setup.

"Oh, man," says Josh, approaching Clark. "I wish you hadn't done that. We're not ready to announce phase two yet."

"Phase two?" asks Clark.

Josh laughs. "As in, you can't have *too* many Metallos!"

Suddenly, multiple doors open around the room and in step multiple Metallos. The identical robots march toward Clark Kent and surround him.

Turn the page.

"You see, Superman can't be everywhere at once," Josh explains. "And neither can Metallo. But with my brains and Lex Luthor's money, we were able to create dozens of Metallos. Soon, crime in Metropolis will be a thing of the past."

Clark scans the surrounding robots. "So, which one is the real Metallo?"

Josh shakes his head. "Oh, none of these." He marches across the large room. "Follow me."

Clark doesn't think he has much of a choice. As he follows the younger man, rows of Metallos march alongside him like guards.

Josh leads them past the rows of Metallo VR pilots and into a brightly lit room. Another Metallo stands frozen in the center of the room, encased in a clear cylinder.

"This is John Corben, the real Metallo," Josh announces. "Mr. Luthor and I used him to design the other robots.

"You're actually keeping him prisoner here?" asks Clark.

"He's a criminal," replies Josh. "He was out of control and has to be locked up somewhere, right?" He strolls over to Metallo and puts a hand on the clear tube. "At least here we can study him."

"When people find out the truth about this . . ." Clark begins.

"Yeah, about that . . ." says Josh. He nods and two Metallo robots grab Clark's arms. "Lock him up," Josh orders. "I have to talk to Mr. Luthor and figure out what to do with you."

The Metallo robots drag Clark out of the room and down another hallway. He could easily use Superman's strength to break free. But if he did, his secret identity of Clark Kent would be blown.

"You'll never get away with this," he says as they toss him into a windowless office. He hears the door lock after they close the door.

Turn the page.

Clark lowers his glasses and scans the room with his X-ray vision. One of the walls leads outside. Luckily, there are no electrical or flammable lines hidden inside. That's all he needs to know.

Clark quickly changes into Superman and then uses his heat vision to cut a large circle through the outside wall.

THUD!

The circle-shaped piece of wall falls into the room.

Suddenly, the door flies open and two Metallos step inside!

"I sent Mr. Kent home," says Superman with his hands on his hips. "But I stuck around to see about your Metallo infestation."

If Superman lures the robots outside, turn to page 70.
If he confronts Josh Bear, turn to page 79.

Superman drops to the ground and runs away from the giant robot. He can no longer fly because of the Kryptonite radiation.

Metallo spots him. "There you are," booms the huge robot. He swipes at Superman with a giant hand, but the super hero leaps over it and keeps running.

Superman sprints toward a large building full of activity. Workers run machinery that crushes and melts down massive amounts of metal. Molten metal glows and sparks fly inside the factory. "If any place has a way to trap a metal giant," says Superman, "this is it."

"Everyone get out!" Superman shouts as he runs through the main doors. "It's not safe. Everyone needs to leave, right now!"

The workers flee the area while Metallo stomps closer. The huge cyborg leans down and peers through the entrance. The doors are too small for him to enter.

Turn the page.

"Think this will keep me out?" Metallo asks with an electronic chuckle.

The giant robot freezes, and its green eyes dim. Like a pilot hopping out of a cockpit, Metallo drops out of the giant robot's chest. Back at his original size, he casually strolls through the open doors.

"I don't know what you expect to do in here, Superman," says Metallo while he looks around the facility. "Crush me inside a giant press? Melt me down in one of those pots? You know this body is almost indestructible."

Superman staggers away from the cyborg. Metallo's Kryptonite heart makes him weaker every second, but he doesn't give up.

With his super-vision, Superman zooms in on the melted metal in a nearby pit. Even in his weakened state, his eyes are stronger than any microscope in the world. He quickly identifies the molten metal. He moves closer to the glowing pit.

"This is getting embarrassing," says Metallo. He leaps into the air and slams down on Superman's back. "It's time to finish you once and for all." He reaches down and flips the super hero over.

Superman groans as he is bathed in the green radiation. He shields his eyes with one hand and reaches back with the other. He dips a hand into the molten metal behind him and scoops up a handful. Then he flings the glowing liquid at Metallo. It splashes across the cyborg's face and chest.

"Ha!" Metallo laughs. "This body cannot be harmed by molten steel." He wipes the red-hot metal from his metallic face.

"Not molten steel," says Superman. "It's lead."

Using his last bit of strength, Superman blasts Metallo with his icy breath. The glowing red metal cools and turns dull gray. The Man of Steel instantly feels better with the Kryptonite encased in a protective layer of lead. It is the only metal that can block the harmful radiation.

Turn the page.

"No!" Metallo tries to wipe away the material, but it's too late. The lead has created a hard layer around his Kryptonite heart.

"Now it's my turn," says Superman. He punches the cyborg so hard that he crashes into the giant junk robot outside. It falls apart around him.

Superman doesn't give the villain time to rebuild the giant robot. He dives into the scrap heap and punches the cyborg again, sending him exploding straight up out of the metal pile. Superman flies after him and meets him in the sky above the city.

"I will destroy you, Superman!" shouts Metallo.

"I think it's time for you to go into sleep mode," says Superman. He reaches in and plucks the lead-coated Kryptonite from the cyborg's chest.

Metallo's green eyes dim, and he begins to fall. Superman catches the cyborg with his free hand.

"I'll find a safe place to take you — *and* this Kryptonite," says Superman.

THE END

To follow another path, turn to page 21.

Superman doesn't have the strength to stand. He stares at the floor and uses the last option left to him. The super hero concentrates his heat vision on the floor. Thin red beams shoot from his eyes and trace a circle on the floor around him. The beams cut through, and Superman falls to the floor below.

"There's nowhere to hide, Superman," Lex Luthor taunts. "This is my building. I know every inch of it."

Superman finds himself in the center of a long hallway. He scrambles to his feet and looks around. "I need a place to recover," he says to himself.

At one end of the hallway, he sees a sign that reads: *Research and Development*. At the other end another sign reads: *Radiation Study*.

If Superman moves to Research and Development, turn to page 77.

If Superman heads toward Radiation Study, turn to page 84.

Superman zips out through the hole in the wall and spins around. "Gentlemen, care to step outside?" he says.

The two Metallos activate their rockets and blast toward the hole. One passes right through, while the other misses completely.

KRASH! It smashes through the wall. Both robots fly toward the Man of Steel.

Superman dodges the first robot and lands a punch on the second.

SMACK! It tumbles backward, slamming into a large billboard.

Superman turns to face the first Metallo robot, but he's too late. A metal fist connects with his jaw.

POW! Superman is knocked back a few feet before recovering. That's when the second Metallo flies back from the billboard.

Superman spins around to avoid the robot's metal grasp. As it flies past, the Man of Steel grabs one of its legs and twirls it around. He uses the robot as a club to smash the other one.

CRUNCH!

POP! TZZZ! TZZ! Sparks fly from the robotic Metallos. Superman swoops up and smashes them together with all of his might.

FOOM! They explode in a ball of fire.

"I'm glad those weren't as tough as the real Metallo," he says. "But fighting more than one is hard work."

Suddenly, there's a roaring sound from below. Superman glances down to see Metallo robots stream out of the building as if someone has kicked a hornet's nest. What looks like dozens of identical robots swarm up to the floating super hero.

Turn to page 73.

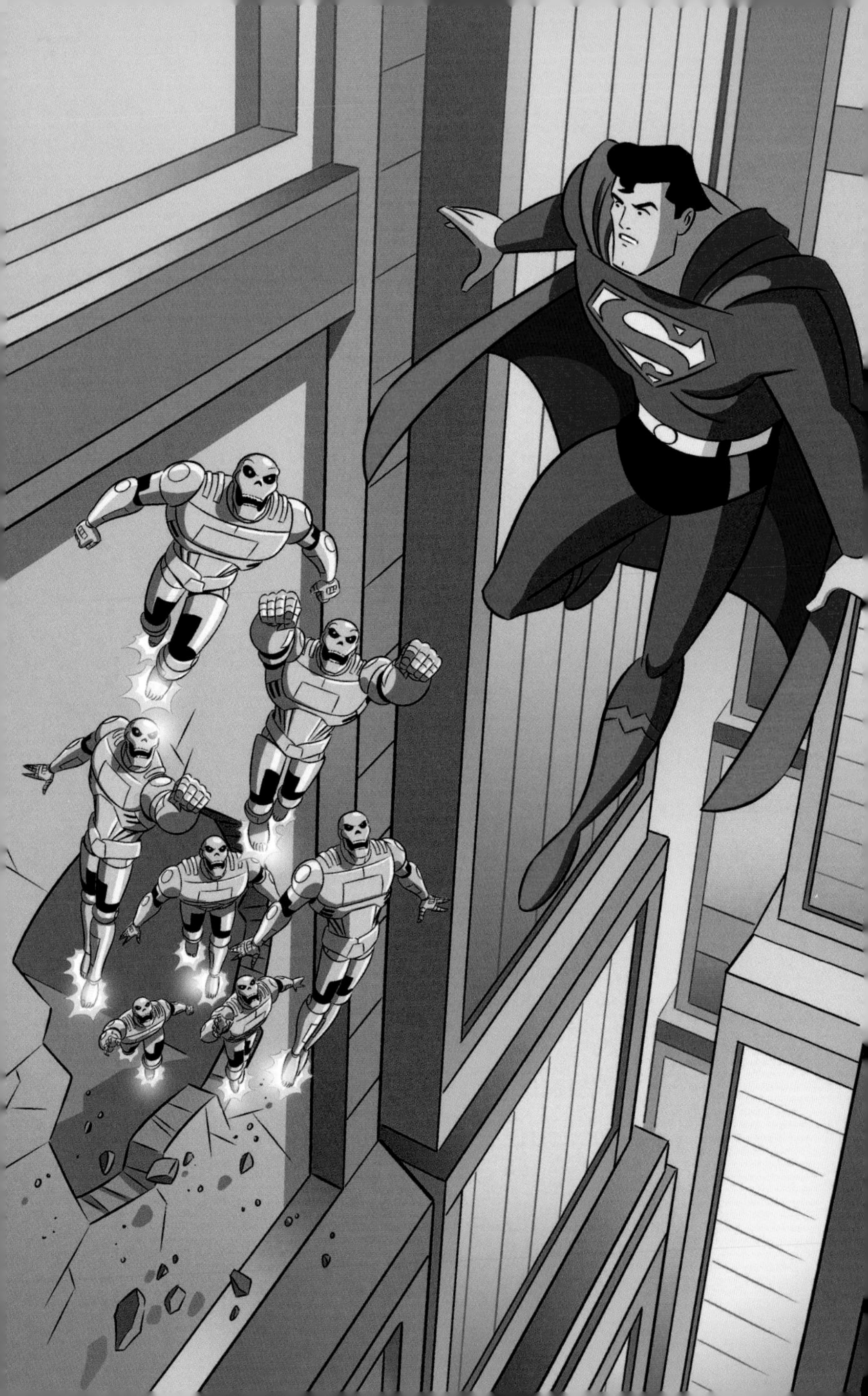

"Uh-oh," says Superman as he dives toward the horde of flying robots. He tightens his fists and reaches them out in front of him. The Man of Steel plows through the approaching enemy. Some robots get knocked away, while some blow up on impact. However, too few are disabled. There are still hundreds to deal with.

"I need a new plan of attack," says Superman.

Superman soars high into the sky and into the clouds. The robots give chase. Once among the clouds, Superman slows down. He can see the robots with his X-ray vision, but they can't see him. He quietly flies through the murky surroundings while they spread out to look for him.

Superman comes up behind three hovering robots. He blasts one with his heat vision while grabbing the other two with each hand.

CRUNCH! He smashes all three together before disappearing back into the clouds.

Turn the page.

Another Metallo disappears as Superman grabs it by the legs and jerks it downward. The super hero uses the robot as a club, bashing it against four more unsuspecting robots. He takes out all five before vanishing into another cloud.

"Batman would be proud of this strategy," Superman says. "But this is taking too long."

One of the robots finds him and latches onto his back. The fake Metallo holds tight with one hand while bashing Superman with the other. The super hero twirls through the air, trying to get rid of his passenger.

When Superman finally flings the robot away, he finds himself underneath the clouds. He's in full view of the Metallo swarm. Before he can hide again, all of the Metallos descend on him from above.

There are too many to fight. The Man of Steel finds himself trapped inside a ball of pounding metal fists and feet.

TZAP! TZAP!

He lashes out with his heat vision, but only a few robots fall away. The small gaps around him quickly fill with more attacking Metallos.

"These things are out of control," Superman says, trying to break free. Then he gets an idea. "Wait a minute. That's it!"

Superman uses his X-ray vision to look through the swarm of Metallos. He concentrates on the Grizzly Games office building. He spots the main power pole just outside the building.

"I can't fight all of these Metallos at once," Superman says. "But I can shut down their controllers."

With all his concentration, Superman ramps up his heat vision. A fine red beam burns through the robot in front of him and then shoots down toward Grizzly Games. The thin beam strikes the large transformer on the power pole.

Turn the page.

TZZ! POP! TZZZZZ!

Sparks fly and electricity dances across the pole. The lights go out through the entire building. With the power gone, all of the Metallos go limp. They stop kicking, punching, and fighting. They simply hover in place.

Superman shoves his way out of the floating mass of robots. "I think it's time to take out the trash."

Using his heat vision once more, Superman fuses the robots together, making a giant ball of Metallos. He grabs the ball and carries it up past the clouds, out of the atmosphere, and into space. With one final shove, he sends the mass of robots hurtling toward the sun.

Superman drops back into the atmosphere and flies toward Grizzly Games. "It's time to put the real Metallo back where he belongs and shut down this Metallo VR game for good."

THE END

To follow another path, turn to page 21.

Superman runs toward the research and development wing. He pushes through double doors to see a wide-open space full of high-tech equipment. The area is littered with half-built tanks, airplane parts, and many things he doesn't recognize.

"Looking for some kind of weapon?" Luthor asks, his voice booming through the company sound system. "I doubt you'll find anything useful. Anyway, by the time you do, Metallo will track you down and destroy you."

The doors open, and Metallo steps inside. His metal feet clank on the floor as he walks in.

"I have to get my strength back before I face him again," Superman says as he ducks behind a row of shelves. "Maybe there's something in here I can use against him." He creeps deeper into the large area.

Turn the page.

Then Superman spots something. One of the workbenches holds a stack of familiar cylinders. They are the same control units as the one he pulled from the fighter jet that morning. A nearby computer shows a remote control app on the screen.

Maybe I can use this computer to reprogram these units, Superman thinks. *There may be a way for me to defeat Metallo without being affected by the Kryptonite.*

"Come out, come out, wherever you are," Lex taunts from the building's loudspeakers. Metallo's metal footsteps grow louder.

Superman taps the keyboard. "Now, whom should I target . . ."

If Superman targets Metallo, turn to page 87.
If Superman targets Lex Luthor, turn to page 99.

One of the Metallos steps forward. "Superman!" it says in an electronic version of Josh Bear's voice. "It really is you. I'm your biggest fan!"

"I'm not so sure about that," says Superman. "If you were, you wouldn't talk to me through one of my biggest villains."

"Aw, don't be like that, Superman," says Josh through Metallo's voice. "Come on. Let me show you what these things can do."

The two Metallos turn and march down the hallway. Superman follows them through a maze of corridors.

"Almost there," Josh says through the Metallo robot. "Too bad Mr. Kent escaped. He would've loved to see this."

"Oh, yes. And I'm sure he would've enjoyed your creepy Metallo voice too," Superman adds sarcastically.

Turn the page.

The two Metallo robots stop in front of a large steel door at the end of a wide hallway. One of them presses buttons on a keypad, and the door slides open. Superman follows them through and enters a huge hangar. Dozens of identical Metallo robots are scattered throughout, along with several pieces of military equipment.

"Now before you say anything, just hear me out," Josh says. His voice is now amplified through a loudspeaker in the hangar. The young man stands in a glass control room at the other end of the huge space. "These robots could seriously help you fight crime. They're almost as strong as the original Metallo. Let me show you what I mean."

Josh presses a button on the control panel, and three robots spring to life. Two of them operate a military machine gun. They fire several rounds at the third Metallo.

BRRAK-AK-AK-AK-AK-AK! The bullets ricochet harmlessly off the robot's chest.

"And that's not all," Josh says. "Check this out."

He pushes another button, and a large tank rolls into view. It aims its cannon at one of the robots and fires.

THOOM! The shell hits the robot dead center, engulfing it in a huge fireball. When the smoke clears, the robot is still standing.

"See what I mean," Josh continues. "They're almost as tough as you."

Superman flies up to the control room and hovers in front of the large glass window. "Look, Josh, I'm flattered that you're a fan and want to help. But we can't have all these robots flying around Metropolis. It's far too dangerous."

"But every one of them is under our control," Josh says. "But that's not it, is it? You still don't think they're powerful enough."

Turn the page.

"That's not true. It's just —" Superman begins.

"I bet you'd like a more hands-on test," interrupts Josh. He presses another button.

Superman barely has time to duck as one of the robots swings a metal pipe at his head.

"Quick, aren't they?" asks Josh.

Another robot activates its rockets and blasts toward the Man of Steel. It slams into Superman and smashes him up against the tank.

"And that's not all," Josh continues. "Check out this little trick I figured out."

Josh presses more buttons, and two of the Metallo robots split up. Each of them marches toward a tank. The robots hop up, land on the tanks, and place their hands on the tanks' large cannons. Their hands melt into the metal, and then they pull the cannons off the tanks. The Metallo robots now have tank cannons for arms.

Both robots then turn and fire on Superman.

KTHOOM! KTHOOM!

The explosions knock Superman across the hangar. He tumbles to a stop across the hard floor. Breathing heavily, the super hero stumbles to his feet.

"And the beauty of it is, I can do this all day," Josh says with a laugh.

If Superman escapes the training facility, turn to page 91.
If he shuts down the training facility, turn to page 102.

Superman runs down the hallway toward the radiation study. Unfortunately, he hears the sound of Metallo's rockets as the cyborg floats down through the hole in the floor.

Superman smashes a keypad by the security door and it slides open. He runs inside.

Once inside, Superman spots something that would be very helpful. He also spots the nearby security camera. The super hero sends a tiny red beam of heat vision its way.

FZZZT! The camera crackles with electricity and melts.

"No fair," says Lex. "I wanted to watch Metallo drain the rest of your powers."

Back upstairs, Lois struggles against the security guards. "Let me go," she demands.

"Not yet," says Luthor. "You'll miss the grand finale." He taps his smartwatch. "I'm having Metallo bring Superman back here, so we can all watch his end together. Ah, here they are now," Luthor says with a chuckle.

Turn to page 86.

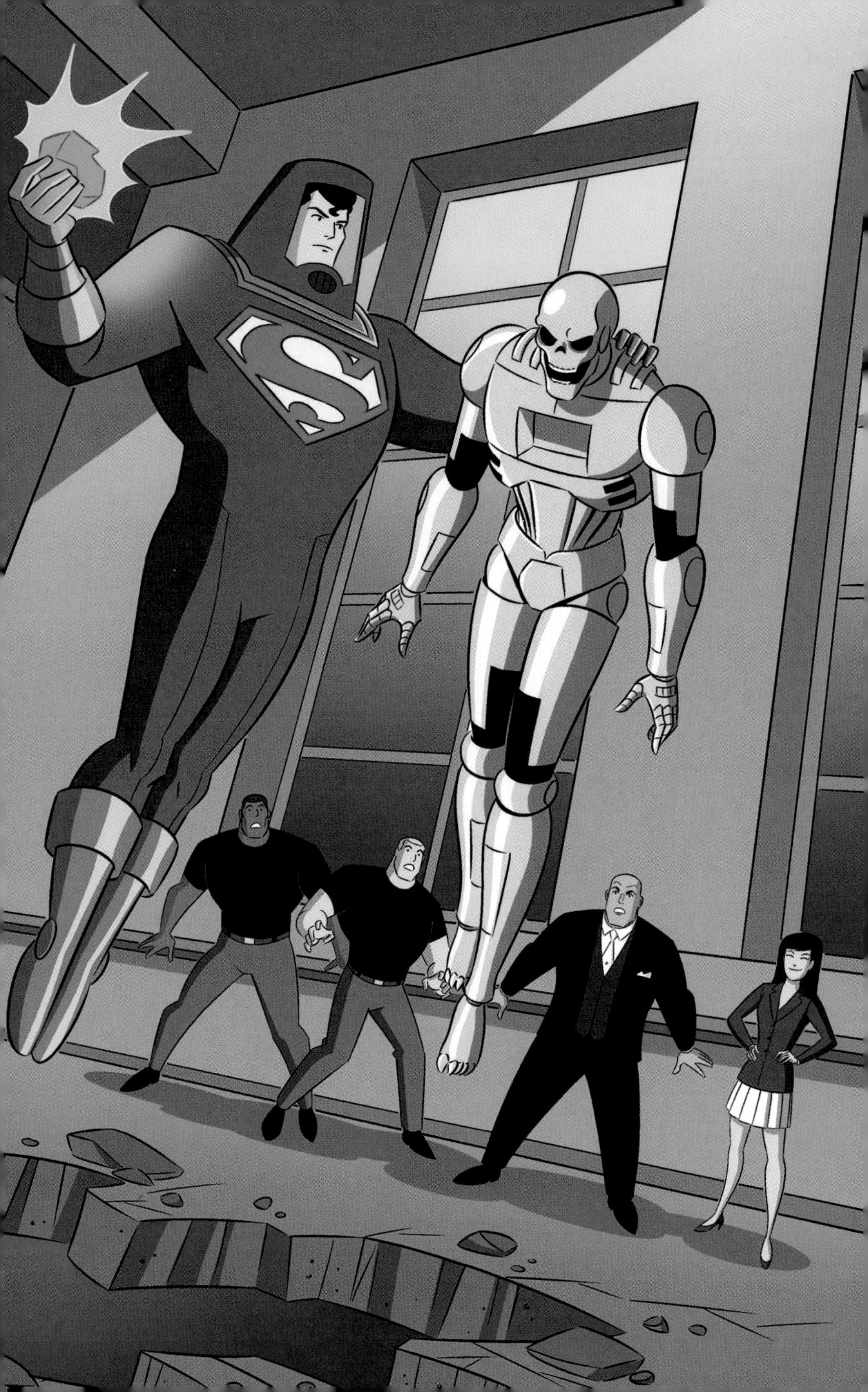

But Luthor is shocked to see Superman carrying Metallo with one arm through the hole in the floor. The Man of Steel wears a protective suit with a clear visor. In his other hand he holds Metallo's Kryptonite heart.

"Nice radiation lab you have down there," Superman says. "Just rows and rows of lead-lined suits. I'm glad to see that you're very concerned about safety here at LexCorp." Superman squeezes his hand around the Kryptonite, smashing it to dust.

Lois shakes off the guards and joins Superman. She looks back at Luthor with a sly smile. "Sorry, Lex. It looks like there's room for only one super hero here in Metropolis."

THE END

To follow another path, turn to page 21.

Superman enters the final command on the computer just as Metallo closes in. The super hero grunts in pain as the Kryptonite radiation hits him once more.

Before the remote-control cyborg gets closer, Superman sprints to the closest window. He grabs a military radio off another workbench before leaping through the window.

KRASH!

Superman focuses his remaining strength on flying out to sea. As he flies, he switches on the radio. "Superman to the *Elissa*," he says into the microphone. "I need to speak with Admiral Jenkins."

"Jenkins here," crackles the speaker a moment later.

"Admiral, you have one more fighter plane with the LexCorp control unit in it, correct?" asks Superman.

Turn the page.

"That's right, Superman," replies the admiral. "But we were about to dismantle it."

"Can you launch it instead?" asks Superman. "Without a pilot?"

"Are you sure?" asks the admiral.

Superman looks back over his shoulder. Metallo is in pursuit. "I'm sure," he replies. "You'll have to trust me."

As Metallo gains on him, Superman can feel the approaching Kryptonite draining him once more. He can also hear Luthor speaking through the cyborg's mouth.

"You're only making this harder on yourself, Superman," Luthor says with Metallo's electronic voice.

Superman ignores the taunts and aims for the large aircraft carrier on the horizon. In the distance, he sees a jet launch from the flight deck. The fighter turns and flies straight for him. When the plane gets closer, it launches two missiles at the Man of Steel.

VRROOOOSH!

Superman swerves out of the way, and the missiles fly past him. They almost hit Metallo instead. The remote-controlled cyborg dodges sideways to avoid the incoming rockets, which explode when they hit the water.

KA-BLAM!

"Very clever," says Luthor "Using my own tech against me and Metallo."

The jet circles around for another attack.

"But you forget how strong I built his body," says Luthor. "It can withstand anything that jet fires at it."

"I know," says Superman. "But I didn't program the plane's control unit to target Metallo."

The fighter jet opens fire once more.

FOOOM!

Superman smiles. "I programmed it to find and target Kryptonite!"

Turn the page.

"NO!" Luthor shouts as the hail of bullets strike Metallo's Kryptonite heart. The glowing rock disappears in a cloud of green dust.

Superman feels better as soon as the rock is destroyed. He swoops down and catches Metallo's limp robotic body before it splashes into the ocean.

Superman holds up the radio. "Admiral, you can call back your fighter jet," he says. "Don't worry. It'll listen to your commands now."

"Will do, Superman," replies the admiral. "But can I ask . . . what was that all about?"

The Man of Steel smiles. "Let's just say that Lex Luthor is finished with the remote control business."

THE END

To follow another path, turn to page 21.

Superman focuses his heat vision on Josh's control panel. But then one of the robots leaps in front of the beam. The Metallo clone is blown to bits.

"There has to be another way to shut down these Metallos," Superman says to himself.

The super hero narrowly dodges another cannon round from the tank-armed robots. Superman takes to the air and flies back to the door where he came in. The thick metal door is sealed, but that's never stopped the Man of Steel. He lands and jams his fingers into the thick metal. He peels back the door as easily as opening a soda can.

"Where you going, Superman?" asks Josh. "There's tons more to show you."

Turn the page.

Superman glances over his shoulder just in time to see two more Metallo robots with cannons for arms. They take aim and blast him at the same time.

KA-VOOOM!

The explosion hurls Superman through the hole in the door and down the long hallway like a bullet through a rifle. He reaches the end of the hall but doesn't stop there. His speed sends him crashing through walls, offices, conference rooms, and more testing areas. He finally comes to a stop when he dents a giant metal breaker box.

The super hero slowly gets to his feet but tenses when he finds another Metallo staring down at him. This one doesn't attack, however. It's not one of the Metallo robots. It is the real Metallo, still sealed inside the clear cylinder.

Superman suddenly hears movement behind him. He spins to see three of the robots crawling through the hole he left in the laboratory wall.

The first robot enters and springs across the room. Superman grabs it by the arm and flings it aside. It crashes into the clear cylinder. Superman then zips over to the other two and grabs their arms before they can pull themselves through. Superman jerks them from the wall and smashes them on the floor.

The first robot recovers and is about to pounce on Superman's back when something grabs it by the neck. It's the real Metallo. The cylinder cracked open during the battle.

"What is this?" Metallo asks in his electronic voice. He examines the squirming robot in his hands. "Is this your doing, Superman?"

Turn the page.

"Like I'd want more of you around," replies the super hero. "No, Corben, you can thank your old pal Lex Luthor for this."

"Luthor!" Metallo shouts as he smashes the phony robot on the ground.

Superman catches his breath. "Oh, yeah. He has a guy named Josh Bear controlling an entire army of these things."

Metallo fixes his green eyes on the Man of Steel. "Where can I find this . . . Josh Bear?"

"Easy," replies Superman. He points to the hole in the wall. "Just follow the path of destruction."

Metallo ignites the rockets in his feet and zooms out of the lab. Superman flies after him as the cyborg makes his way to the training area. When the two enter the large hangar, dozens more robots stand ready for battle.

"Just couldn't keep away. Huh, Superman?" Josh asks. He glances at Metallo and then down to his control board. He leans close to a microphone. "Say, who's operating the Metallo that just flew in with Superman? Naveen? Brandon?"

"No one operates *me*, boy!" Metallo booms in his electronic voice.

Josh's eyes widen. "Oh . . . th . . . this is bad." He flicks switches on the control panel. "Bad, bad, bad." Josh leans toward the mic. "All operators, we have a code four. I repeat, code four!"

Suddenly, all the robots attack Superman and the real Metallo. The super hero and the cyborg super-villain fight back-to-back, fending off a swarm of punching, kicking, and blasting robots.

Superman sends out a beam of heat vision, cutting through ten of the robots at once. Metallo grabs one robot by the ankles and uses it as a club. He destroys fifteen robots before the one he holds falls apart.

Turn the page.

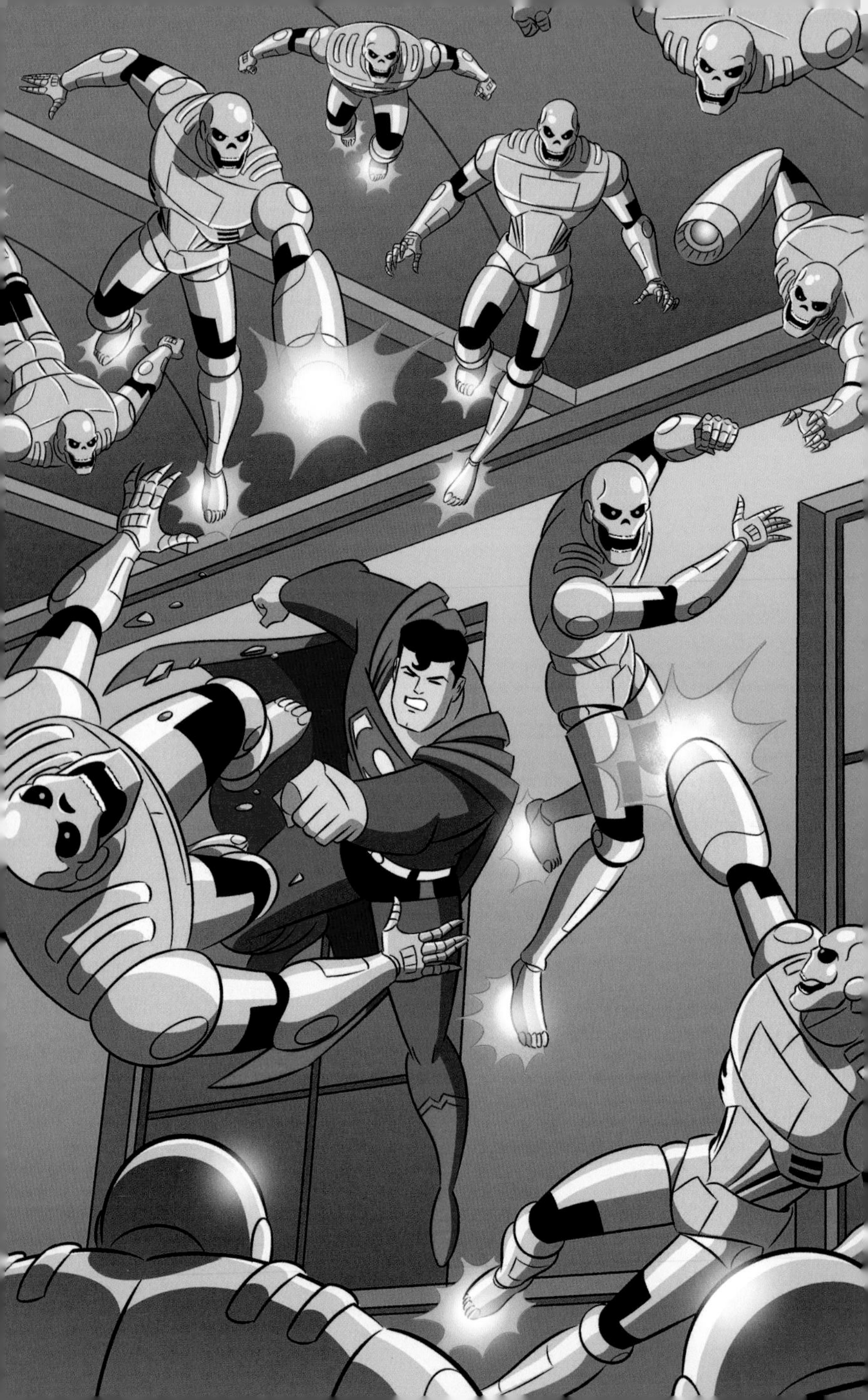

Superman blasts four more robots with his freeze-breath and then shatters them with a single punch. Metallo punches his way through six more of the robot copies.

KTHOOM! KTHOOM!

The robots with the morphed weapons attack in force. The Man of Steel and the man of metal dodge the attack and then lunge after the cannon robots. Metallo turns one cannon robot so it fires on the others.

KA-THOOM! The cannon blasts them into pieces. Metallo smashes the last one before its cannon can reload. Meanwhile, Superman bends the barrel arm of a robot before punching it to pieces.

In the end, Superman and Metallo stand alone amid piles of smoking robot parts. Metallo looks up at the control booth, beaming his glowing green eyes at Josh Bear. "You!"

Metallo slowly rises toward the booth. Josh yips and ducks under the control panel.

Turn the page.

Superman zips in front of him, blocking his way. "I can't let you hurt anyone, Corben."

"After what he did to me?" asks Metallo.

"I'll make sure he answers for his crimes," Superman says while crossing his arms. "You should too."

Metallo laughs. "Maybe some other time." The cyborg looks up and blasts toward the ceiling. He crashes through and disappears into the sky.

Superman hovers closer to the control booth and shakes his head.

Josh climbs out from under the panel. He gives Superman a thumbs-up. "Still your biggest fan!"

"Yeah, thanks," replies Superman. "But it's time you found a new hobby. Luckily, you'll have plenty of time in prison to do just that."

THE END

To follow another path, turn to page 21.

Superman finishes typing and snatches two of the control units from the workbench. He ducks down another aisle as Metallo steps forward.

"What are your plans for those?" Luthor asks.

"Just a little research and development of my own," Superman replies. He grabs two drones from another workbench and sprints down another aisle.

Metallo's footsteps grow louder as Luthor moves the cyborg closer. Superman feels weaker as the Kryptonite nears.

"There's nowhere left to run," Luthor announces with a laugh.

Metallo cuts off Superman's escape, backing the super hero into a corner. Superman is almost out of strength. He plugs the control units into the drones and switches them on. The drones' propellers whir to life, and the two machines float out of his hands. They fly straight for Metallo.

"What is this pathetic attempt?" asks Luthor.

"It's called improvising," replies Superman.

Turn the page.

The drones fly past the remote-controlled cyborg. They buzz out of the lab and into the long hallway. Both drones rise up through the hole in the ceiling and into Lex Luthor's office. They swoop after the bald man.

Luthor ducks, and they narrowly miss striking his bald head. "Guards!" he growls. "Do something!"

The security guards release Lois and begin swatting at the large drones. The machines buzz just out of reach.

Lois sees her chance and makes another grab for Luthor's smartwatch. This time she succeeds. She snatches it from Luthor's wrist and taps in her own commands. A floor below, the hatch on Metallo's chest closes, and he stops moving. Superman gives a sigh of relief as his strength begins to return.

Superman grabs the frozen Metallo and flies back up to Luthor's office. Luthor and the guards are still fending off the attacking drones.

"Thanks for your help, Lois," Superman says. "I'll take Metallo somewhere safe. Need a lift?"

"Sure," Lois replies. She twirls the watch around one finger. "And it's nice saving you for a change."

As Superman carries Lois and Metallo out of Luthor's office, the three men continue swatting at the attacking drones.

"What do I pay you two for?" asks Luthor. "Get them!"

"We're trying, Mr. Luthor," says the taller guard. "We're trying!"

THE END

To follow another path, turn to page 21.

I have to get up there and stop him, Superman thinks to himself.

KTHOOM! A direct hit from one robot's arm cannon sends the Man of Steel hurtling across the hangar. He slams into the wall and falls to the ground. Breathing hard, he scrambles to his feet.

"That kind of firepower is probably nothing to you, huh?" asks Josh. "Well, check this out."

Ten Metallo robots swarm to the one with a cannon for an arm. When they separate, all ten now have tank cannons in place of their right arms.

"The robots can copy each other," Josh explains. "Cool idea, huh?"

The newly-modified robots turn toward Superman and fire.

FOOM! FOOM! FOOM! FOOM! FOOM!

The super hero zigzags around the large hangar, dodging the many explosions.

"Call them off, Josh," Superman orders.

"What's the fun in that?" asks Josh.

Superman flies toward the control room. "Does it look like I'm having fun to you?"

Josh looks up and his eyes widen. The Metallos are shooting at Superman, who is flying directly at him. The young man reaches for the controls, but it's too late.

KTHOOM! KTHOOM!

Two of the shots zip past Superman and blast the control room. Josh dives for cover as the glass shatters and the control panel erupts in flames.

KRASH! KA-VOOM!

All of the Metallos in the training area suddenly go limp. Those that were hovering crash to the ground. The rest crumple where they stand.

"Josh!" Superman shouts as he flies up to what's left of the room.

"Ha-ha-ha-ha-ha!" Josh's laugh drifts up from the debris. Only his voice has a robotic quality, almost electronic.

Turn the page.

A steel beam moves aside, and a figure rises from the rubble. The mask that was Josh Bear's face is torn, revealing glowing eyes underneath.

"Josh?" asks Superman. "No, it can't be."

"Not Josh," says an electronic voice. "John. John Corben."

Superman frowns. "Metallo."

"You've made quite a mess of my metal army," the cyborg says. "Now I'll have to find another way to get my revenge."

"Not if I can help it," Superman replies.

"Easy now." Metallo opens the hatch on his chest. "I'm the one with the Kryptonite heart, remember?" Superman staggers back as the radiation washes over him.

Metallo activates the rockets on his feet and rises off the floor. "We'll meet again, Superman," the cyborg says as he rises into the air. "You never know where or who I'll be." He blasts through the roof and flies into the sky

THE END

To follow another path, turn to page 21.

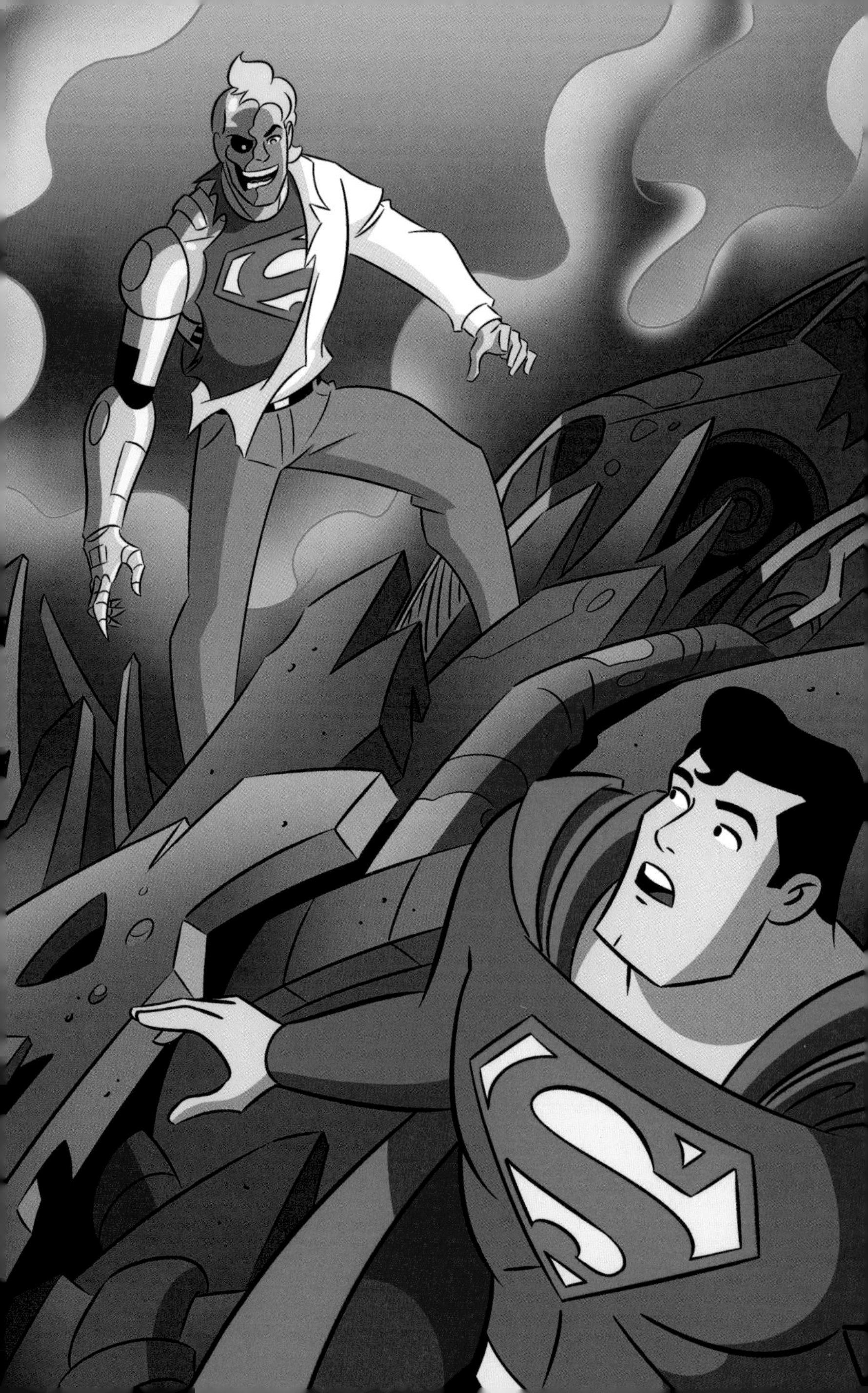

AUTHOR

Michael Anthony Steele has been in the entertainment industry for more than 24 years writing for television, movies, and video games. He has authored more than one hundred books for exciting characters and brands, including Batman, Green Lantern, Shrek, LEGO City, Spider-Man, Tony Hawk, Word Girl, Garfield, Night at the Museum, and The Penguins of Madagascar. Mr. Steele lives on a ranch in Texas, but he enjoys meeting his readers when he visits schools and libraries all over the country. He can be contacted through his website, MichaelAnthonySteele.com

ILLUSTRATOR

Darío Brizuela was born in Buenos Aires, Argentina, in 1977. He enjoys doing illustration work and character design for several companies, including DC Comics, Marvel Comics, Image Comics, IDW Publishing, Titan Publishing, Hasbro, Capstone Publishers, and Disney Publishing Worldwide. Darío's work can be found in a wide range of properties, including *Star Wars Tales*, *Ben 10*, *DC Super Friends*, *Justice League Unlimited*, *Batman: The Brave & The Bold*, *Transformers*, *Teenage Mutant Ninja Turtles*, *Batman 66*, *Wonder Woman 77*, *Teen Titans Go!*, *Scooby Doo! Team Up*, and *DC Super Hero Girls*.

GLOSSARY

artificial intelligence (ar-ti-FISH-uhl in-TEL-uh-junss)—the ability of a machine to think and act like a person

buoy (BOO-oy)—a floating marker in a body of water

cockpit (KOK-pit)—the area in the front of an airplane where the pilot sits

cyborg (SY-borg)—a being that is a combination of both organic and mechanical parts

cylinder (SI-luhn-duhr)—a shape with flat, circular ends and sides shaped like a tube

dismantle (diss-MAN-tuhl)—to take something apart

electromagnet (i-lek-troh-MAG-nuht)—a temporary magnet created when an electric current flows through a conductor

harbor (HAR-bur)—a place where ships load and unload passengers and cargo

infestation (in-fes-TAY-shun)—a group of pests that can cause damage or harm

press conference (PRESS KON-fur-uhnss)—a gathering at which public figures answer questions from reporters

radiation (ray-dee-AY-shuhn)—tiny particles sent out from radioactive material

virtual reality (VUR-choo-uhl ree-AL-uh-tee)—a 3D world created by a computer where things on screen seem to be real and come to life

METALLO

Real Name:
John Corben

Occupation:
**criminal and
super-villain**

Base:
Metropolis

Height:
6 feet 5 inches

Weight:
200 pounds

Eyes:
green

Hair:
brown

Metallo was a criminal once employed by Lex Luthor. While in prison, Luthor infected Corben with a deadly disease. To save himself, Corben agreed to an experimental medical procedure. When he woke, he felt unimaginably strong. But to his horror he discovered that his brain had been placed into a cyborg body powered by green Kryptonite. Unable to feel anything but the cold embrace of metal, Corben developed an evil side, making him a major threat to all of Metropolis. Now known as Metallo, he is nearly as strong and fast as the Man of Steel.

- Metallo's heart is made of pure Kryptonite, which powers his exoskeleton. Without the alien mineral, Corben's cyborg body would be completely powerless.

- When the man of metal clashes with the Man of Steel, sparks really fly! Metallo is capable of stunning Superman with his powerful cyborg punches. And by opening his chest-plate, Metallo can bathe Superman in the lethal radiation from his Kryptonite heart.

- Corben was simply a pawn in Luthor's scheme to create a super-villain capable of defeating Superman. Upon discovering the truth, Metallo swore to destroy Luthor for transforming him into a metallic monster.

- Corben has grown used to his metal body, giving him the ability to transform any machinery around him into part of his own exoskeleton!

←YOU CHOOSE→

SUPERMAN

10+ POSSIBLE ENDINGS!